House of the Dead

**This is the third book in the
OTHER WORLD Series**

Other books in the series are:

OCTOBER MOON

GEMINI GAME

both by Michael Scott

MOONLIGHT

by Michael Carroll

This series is a collection of books telling about
out-of-the-ordinary happenings – horror stories,
science fiction, fantasy. Here you will find sharp,
lively events and modern teenage characters, as
well as the strange and mysterious.

**Prepare to be thrilled!
And prepare to be *terrified*!**

Michael Scott

Born and brought up in Dublin, Michael Scott has spent all his life with books. He worked in various bookshops and was an antiquarian bookseller before turning to writing. His first book was published in 1981, and he has had up to fifty books published to date.

He writes for children, teenagers and adults, and his books for young readers include stories from Celtic mythology, fairy tales and fantasy, horror and the supernatural. He has been published in many countries and many of his books have been translated.

The *Irish Guide to Children's Books* praised Michael for his 'unparalleled contribution to children's literature'.

Also by Michael Scott:

OCTOBER MOON

GEMINI GAME

WINDLORD

EARTHLORD

THE SEVEN TREASURES

THE LAST OF THE FIANNA

and many more – check with your bookseller

HOUSE OF
THE DEAD

Michael Scott

THE O'BRIEN PRESS
DUBLIN

First published 1993 by The O'Brien Press Ltd.,
20 Victoria Road, Rathgar, Dublin 6, Ireland

10 9 8 7 6 5 4 3 2 1

British Library Cataloguing-in-publication Data
Scott, Michael
House of the Dead. – (Other World Series)
I. Title II. Series
823.914 [J]

ISBN 0-86278-339-9

Typesetting, editing, design and layout: The O'Brien Press
Cover illustration: Peter Haigh
Cover design: Neasa ní Chianáin
Cover separations: Lithoset, Dublin
Printing: Cox & Wyman, Reading

DEDICATION

for Neasa!

Prologue

Beneath the House of the Dead, the creature waits. And it is patient, for it knows not the meaning of time.

When we put the creature into the ground, we bound it there with carved stone and cold soil. Then we raised the earth atop the cairn, and wove into the fabric of the place a spell to keep the beast at bay.

We knew it was not dead, for that which does not live cannot die.

We knew it was waiting, festering in the earth.

Beneath the House of the Dead, the creature waits.

And it hungers.

Chapter One

Claire Holland dug her hands into the pockets of her 501's and shook her head doubtfully. "I'm not sure," she said, turning to face the window.

Patrick Elliot said nothing, waiting patiently, watching her reflection in the glass as the minibus bounced along the narrow country road. When he saw her lips curl in a wicked smile, he knew she'd do it.

"If we get caught we'll be in deep trouble. We might even get expelled," she said.

"But we can't be expelled in the week of the Christmas holidays, can we?"

She shook her head slowly. "Probably not," she agreed.

"So, do we do it?" Patrick asked, his dark eyes sparkling.

Claire nodded. Reaching out, she squeezed the boy's hand as the creaking minibus came to a halt. "Let's do it!"

Carol Lee pulled off her gloves and clapped her hands, the sound sharp and piercing in the chill December air. One by one the class gathered around, stamping their feet, tucking cold hands into armpits, their breaths smoking whitely on the early-morning air.

Miss Lee stood on her toes and did a quick count, trying to see over the heads of her students, most of whom were taller than her. "Claire! Patrick! Would you care to join us – *please*?"

Patrick and Claire were standing a little apart from the rest of the class, leaning up against the bonnet of the school minibus.

"It's warmer here, Miss," Claire said. She tapped the engine.

"It would be even warmer inside the bus," Patrick murmured, just loud enough for those at the back of the group to hear. There was a scatter of giggles.

Miss Lee exhaled in a great gushing sigh. Folding her arms, she tapped her foot until the two reluctantly moved away from the bus and joined the rest of the group. The teacher glanced at her watch. "We don't have much time." She turned and pointed to the enormous white-walled circular mound that rose out of the low hill, wisps of grey mist curling around its base. "Pay attention. Behind us is Newgrange. This is the oldest engineered building on the planet. It was built approximately three thousand years before the birth of Christ, making it older than Stonehenge, older than the Great Pyramid of Cheops. It is neolithic in origin, and was created using only the simplest of tools."

"No JCB's then?" Patrick Elliot said softly, glancing at Claire, but his voice carried on the still air, and all the heads turned in his direction.

"No, Patrick," Miss Lee said icily, "no JCBs, no tractors, no diggers, no shovels. Just simple men using simple tools. Perhaps, Patrick, you would like to tell us what you know of Newgrange."

"Newgrange ..." Patrick said slowly.

"Yes, Patrick. Newgrange. You did want to come here, didn't you?"

"Oh yes, Miss, I wanted to come."

"Well, now that you're here, perhaps you could pay a little more attention. As part of your project, you were supposed to do some research into the history of Newgrange. Would you like to tell us what you discovered?"

"Yes, Miss." Patrick dug his hands into the pockets of his leather jacket, and turned to look at the mound. In the early-morning light, his face looked unnaturally pale, and his circular glasses reflected the grey light. Taking a deep breath, he began, "Newgrange consists of a circle of standing stones, surrounding a huge man-made mound of approximately eighty metres. It is roughly fifteen metres high. The mound was constructed of layers of turves and stones erected over a stone chamber, which is accessible through a long passage lined with standing stones ..."

"That's enough, Patrick," Miss Lee said hurriedly. "It seems you did do some work."

"Yes, Miss, I did," he said, keeping a straight face.

The small nervous woman turned back to look at the mound. "We're here this morning for a unique experience. As you know, every year during the winter solstice, the sun shines through an opening in the mound called a light-box and illuminates the interior at dawn for four days. Visitors come from all over the world to see this phenomenon. However, in recent years the Office of Public Works has been limiting the number of people they allow into the mound due to the damage they cause." She turned and smiled quickly. "Today, we will be the only group there and, I've been told, ours may very well be one of the last groups allowed inside this century. We are very privileged." The smile faded as she glanced over the fourteen students. She was looking at Patrick and Claire when she said, "I trust you will all behave yourselves once we're inside."

"They're opening the gate, Miss," one of the girls said.

Patrick was lifting his arm to look at his watch when Claire said, "It's eight-thirty."

"I imagined it would be darker," Patrick said, looking around. It had been brightening for the past thirty minutes and now the sky was silver and grey with the dawn. The brightest of the night stars still glittered in the heavens.

"Sunrise is at around ten to nine," Claire said, her voice muffled and distant. She had wrapped a thick woollen scarf around her head and across her mouth. Strands of soft brown hair curled around her square face, now pale with the chill, emphasising her deep brown eyes.

"So what do we do – hang around here for the next twenty minutes?" Patrick clapped his gloved hands together, trying to bring feeling back to his fingers, and stamped his feet. Frost crackled on the grass. "I'm freezing," he added miserably.

"You should have worn warmer clothing," Claire said, glancing at Patrick's threadbare jeans and scarred leather jacket.

"I did. These were all I could find," he said. "At least I've gloves." He lifted his hands, displaying a pair of gloves that were at least one size too small.

"It'll be warmer inside the mound," Claire said gently. She knew that neither Patrick's father nor his mother had worked for over two years, and that finances were stretched in the Elliot household.

"Hurry up, you two!" Miss Lee called. The students were walking in a ragged line towards the ancient mound. Patrick and Claire took up positions at the back of the queue.

"Are you sure you want to do this?" Patrick asked.

"Why? Are you having second thoughts?" Claire teased.

"Me! No," he said quickly. He nodded to the opening. "We'll wait until everyone is inside and then we'll slip out."

"She'll know it's us," Claire muttered, nodding towards Miss Lee.

"Not if we go back in immediately afterwards."

Claire dipped her head as she ducked into the narrow passageway. "One of these days, Patrick Elliot," she said quietly, "you and I are going to get into real trouble."

"But not today," Patrick grinned.

The icy mist swirled and curled, twisting into coiling shapes and patterns. Delicate silver water droplets covered everything, highlighting the countless spider's webs blanketing the bushes that bordered the fields.

The bushes shook, the silvered webs shattering like broken glass, and from the concealment of the leaves cold grey eyes watched the class disappear into the ancient House of the Dead.

Chapter Two

It felt their presence.

It felt the heat of their bodies, heard their breaths wheezing in their lungs, heard their blood hissing through their veins.

Human-kind.

Soft-skinned, weak-minded.

Human-kind.

It tested its bonds, those chains of stone and soil and light, and found that they were still strong.

It waited.

And it hungered.

It hungered.

Chapter Three

Patrick slipped out of the mound and back into the chill morning air. Claire scrambled after him, bending her head to creep through the low opening. They both crouched at the entrance, listening intently, half-expecting to hear Miss Lee call their names. Echoing faintly out of the dark entrance that led deep into the heart of the mound, they could hear their teacher's voice bouncing off the carved stones.

"... the first rays of sunlight will stream through the light-box over the entranceway and illuminate this inner ..."

"Quick," Patrick said, unzipping his leather jacket and pulling it off, "we don't have much time left. The sun's about to rise. Give me your coat."

While her gloved fingers fumbled with her buttons, Claire turned to the east. The band of grey-white clouds low on the horizon was now rimmed with orange and deep bronze. Pulling off her gloves with her teeth, she unbuttoned the heavy coat, shrugged it off and tossed it to Patrick.

"You watch the sun," he said.

Tucking both coats under one arm, he hauled himself up

on to the flat stone above the low door.

"Any second now!" Claire called.

Shoving his own jacket into the square window-like opening above the door, Patrick spread it out, covering as much of the opening as he could.

"Patrick ..." Claire said warningly as the edge of the clouds turned yellow and gold.

Gripping Claire's coat tightly in both hands, Patrick spread it across the rest of the opening, completely covering the light-box ... just as the first rays of sunrise touched the edge of the stone. He grinned, showing strong white teeth: the sun would not shine into Newgrange this year!

Carol Lee glanced at the luminous dial of her watch, the hands and numerals glowing green in the gloom. "Any second now," she announced, her hushed voice echoing in the chamber. She could just about make out the shapes of the class moving around her, shuffling nervously, awed by the interior of the ancient mound. "We are about to witness an event that has taken place every year, beginning almost three thousand years before the birth of Christ ..."

The teacher looked at her watch again. According to the newspaper, the sun would rise at eight-forty-eight.

It was now eight-forty-nine. Maybe her watch was slow.

She cleared her throat. "I want you to try and imagine what the primitive men who built this place must have thought when they saw the sun slicing through the night to light up the interior of this mound. Remember, they worshipped the sun as a god, they believed in magic, and ..."

Someone started whispering.

"Silence!" she snapped.

The low insistent whispering continued.

"Stop that whispering. Patrick Elliot, Claire Holland, stop it at once." She was only guessing that they were the culprits, but she knew they were usually at the heart of any trouble-making.

Eight-fifty.

The whispering intensified, the words almost distinguishable, the syllables rasping, almost like a beast's growling.

"Stop that noise immediately," she snapped, but she was surprised to find that her voice was shaking. Carol Lee dug in her pocket, pulled out a torch and snapped it on, the sudden light taking everyone – including herself – by surprise. The small group threw up their hands to protect their eyes. "Patrick Elliot ..." she began as the torch moved from face to face. And stopped. Patrick Elliot wasn't in the chamber. Nor was Claire Holland.

The whispering was louder now.

It was coming from behind her ... but there was nothing behind her except solid rock ... and now she could feel the noise trembling up from beneath her feet, the dusty earth vibrating with the sounds, the dry soil shivering into twisted circular patterns.

It was like a man shouting.

It was like a beast snarling.

And then the whispering turned to laughter.

Triumphant, victorious laughter.

"What was that?" Claire stooped to peer into the darkened doorway.

"I don't know," Patrick said slowly. He too thought he'd heard something.

The girl glanced back over her shoulder. The sun had risen in the east, bathing the side of the mound in warm golden light, while blinding reflections danced from the chunks of quartz set into the white walls. She looked up at Patrick who was still standing on the flat stone above the door. The sunlight had drained the colour from his skin, making him look even paler than usual, his glasses reflecting the light, like small circular mirrors. "It sounded like laughter ..." she said slowly.

Patrick nodded. It *had* sounded like laughter.

"That's enough, Patrick. Let's give it up."

"Just another minute," he insisted, checking to ensure that the opening was completely covered and no light was leaking into the mound. "I'd love to be able to see their faces. I can just see Lee in there, going on and on about the sun coming in through the light-box, and that this is something that has been happening for thousands of years. She'll probably want an essay about it." He screwed up his face and imitated Miss Lee's high-pitched voice. "Now I want an essay, four foolscap pages, nothing less, about the ..."

Shrill and terrifying, the high-pitched scream sliced through the early-morning air, echoing off the walls, magnified by the stones.

"What ...?" Claire whispered.

"It came from inside." Tossing the girl's coat down, he pulled his own jacket out of the opening and climbed off the flat stone.

Claire leaned into the entrance, turning her head to one

side and pulling her thick brown hair off her ear. "I can't hear anything."

Patrick tugged his coat on and crouched beside her, squinting into the darkness. He wrinkled his nose. "Do you smell anything?"

Claire breathed deeply. "No ... yes! Bitter, like lemons."

Patrick shook her head. "No, it's like sour milk."

Claire crouched down beside the boy and put her hand on his shoulder. "Listen," she whispered.

He shook his head. "I don't hear anything."

"Exactly." She looked at Patrick, her brown eyes wide and frightened. "Where are the voices? We should be hearing their voices."

"Hello?" Patrick called into the darkness. "Hello?" He suddenly jerked his head back. The acrid odour of sour milk had intensified. His stomach twisted and he tasted bitter bile at the back of his throat. Rubbing his hand across his stinging eyes, Patrick pulled Claire away from the opening. "It's like some sort of gas ..."

"Like that gas that collects in old mines."

"Methane," Patrick said. "But that's odourless. That's why they brought canaries down into the mines. When the birds died, the miners knew there was a gas leak." His shook his head. "It's not methane."

Claire stood up, shading her eyes against the low sunshine. "We've got to get help." She looked around, but the fields surrounding the ancient monument were empty, and the school bus was the only vehicle in the car park.

Patrick ducked his head into the opening and breathed quickly. "The smell doesn't seem so strong now." Pulling off his scarf, he wrapped it around his mouth and nose. "Stay here." His voice was muffled. "I'll go in and see what's happened."

Claire shook her head. "I'm not staying here on my own. I'm coming in with you," she said firmly, tugging her scarf up around her mouth.

Patrick stepped into the mouth of the tunnel and stopped, blinking hard, giving his eyes time to adjust to the gloom. He could still smell traces of the bitter odour through the scarf. The smell puzzled him; it was vaguely familiar, like the smell from one of the elements in a science experiment ... the one which smelt like rotten eggs.

Claire dropped her hand onto his shoulder, startling him. "Come on," she urged.

"Wish I had a torch," Patrick muttered. Digging in his pockets, he pulled out a battered book of matches. 'These will have to do.' Fumbling the match-book open, he tore off a match and struck it alight. The sharp smell of sulphur helped clear the air, throwing flickering shadows across the sloping walls, bringing the curling symbols and intricate spirals carved into the stone to life.

It took three matches to reach the inner chamber.

The light of the fourth match revealed the bodies of their teacher and classmates.

Chapter Four

"They're dead!" Claire breathed in a horrified whisper. Patrick knelt and scooped up Miss Lee's torch before the match burned down to scorch his fingers. Flicking it on, he played it around the chamber. He was shaking so badly that the beam was dancing wildly. The bodies of the twelve pupils and their teacher lay motionless where they had fallen. Whatever had struck had knocked them down without warning.

"Hold the light steady," Claire snapped, kneeling beside Miss Lee. Turning the teacher's head gently – there was a bruise on her cheekbone where she had struck the ground – Claire pressed the first two fingers of her right hand to the teacher's slender throat. There was a single terrifying moment when she was unable to find any movement, but then she felt the solid throb of a pulse beneath the skin. "She's alive," she breathed. A wave of relief washed over her.

She moved on to the girl who lay beside Miss Lee. It was Jenny French. She had broken her arm in a riding accident recently and her cast was covered in signatures. Claire lifted the girl's broken arm out from beneath her body, and the girl moaned audibly. Claire moved to the next figure. It was Tommy Butler. He lived next door to Patrick and they were great friends. When she pressed a hand to his throat, she could feel a pulse beating strongly. "I think they're all okay," she said, looking up at Patrick and shading her eyes against the torchlight. "That gas we smelt must have knocked them out."

"We need to get them out of here," Patrick said shakily. His heart was hammering violently against his ribs, and he knew he would never forget that first image of the bodies lying scattered across the floor.

Claire shook her head immediately. "I'm not sure we should move them. Some of them may have injured themselves when they fell. I think we should leave them here and go and get help."

"We can't just walk away and leave them," Patrick protested. "What happens if they wake up?"

"I wasn't suggesting that we both simply walk off," Claire snapped. "One of us will have to go to the nearest town – Slane, I think – and find help. The other will stay here to watch over the ..." She stopped, realising that she'd been about to say 'bodies'.

"I'll go," Patrick said immediately. He saw the knowing look in Claire's eyes; she was aware that he was afraid and wanted to get out of the mound. "I can take the school bus," he added. "I'll be there in a few minutes."

"But you can't drive," Claire reminded him.

"I can. I just haven't passed my test." He swung the torch beam around, examining the high ceiling, the stone walls, looking for cracks. "I wonder where the gas came from?" he said, changing the subject.

"Decomposing vegetation maybe, a pocket of gas that seeped up from underground. Isn't this a limestone region? Limestone is porous." She stood up and brushed off her knees. "Look, you'd better hurry. And leave me the torch!"

Patrick looked at the torch in his hand.

"Use your matches," Claire added, before he could ask the question.

Handing the torch to the girl, he pulled the match-book out of his pocket and tore off a match. Brushing strands of fine hair off his forehead, he looked around the chamber again. "Maybe you should wait outside ... just in case there's more gas," he said lamely.

Claire grinned. "Why, Patrick Elliot, don't tell me you're worried about me?"

Without making a reply, Patrick ducked his head and disappeared down the opening. Moments later, his voice echoed back, broken and distorted by the stones. "I'll be back as soon as I can."

"You'd better be," Claire said with feeling.

Propping the torch up in a shallow bowl at the back of the chamber, Claire busied herself trying to make her classmates comfortable, while being careful not to move them too much. Some of them had fallen badly, and were cut and bruised. Martin Simms's bottom lip was torn and bloody and the right lens in his glasses was cracked; and Claire was sure that Helen Lawlor had broken her wrist, it was twisted at such an unusual angle.

When she'd done what she could, the girl sat on the ground with her back to the wall, facing the opening through which she could see the distant rectangle of blue sky. There was nothing she could do now but wait. But where was Patrick? What was keeping him? When she glanced at her watch she was astonished to discover that he'd only been gone seven minutes.

The torch flickered, the beam dimming perceptibly.

Claire shook it, and it brightened again. She moved it across her friends' faces, wondering if anyone was regaining consciousness again. Tommy Butler was twitching slightly, legs trembling as if he was dreaming about running. When she shone the light on his face, she could see that his eyeballs were moving rapidly behind closed lids; REM, it was called, Rapid Eye Movement, a sure sign that the sleeper was dreaming. She wondered what he was dreaming about ...

Whispering ...

The sound shocked her motionless. It sounded like hissing sand, rasping leaves, crackling paper.

Whispering ...

"Patrick? Patrick? Is that you?"

Whispering ...

She attempted to concentrate on the sound, but her heart was thumping so hard she found it difficult to focus on anything else. She could hear whispers – hissing, sighing, rasping whispers, the words almost but not quite distinguishable.

Maybe it was Patrick returning with some help – it was simply their voices echoing across the fields ...

"Leave …"

The torch flickered once, twice, then died to an orange pinprick. The only light now was the distant rectangle that showed the position of the light-box above the door. And it seemed very far away. Her hands began to shake.

"Leave!"

Claire jumped, then started to shiver uncontrollably. Even though she was surrounded by the still bodies of her friends, she felt so alone, so lonely. She opened her mouth to say something, simply to hear a sound in the mound, a real sound, but her mouth was dry, her throat closed, and she couldn't speak.

She took a deep breath, tasting the final residue of the gas in the air. Her mind must be playing tricks on her. Well, she hadn't had a lot of sleep last night, she'd been up early and she'd missed breakfast. She was hearing her own blood rushing in her veins, nothing more, the hiss of her hair across her ears, the distant wind on the stones …

Then she heard it again.

"Leave this …"

She slapped the torch into the palm of her hand. The light flared for a moment, blinding her, then died, plunging the tomb into darkness, except for the perfect orange circles of light that danced before her eyes. Claire put her hand to her mouth to stifle a scream and bit into the inside of her cheek, fighting desperately to remain calm. She sat frozen to the spot on the cold ground.

"Leave this place."

She could make out words now.

"Leave this place!"

She could hear the voice, soft and rasping, like a snake's hiss. The words were in the air all around her, bouncing off the walls, trembling off the ancient carved stones, quivering up through the ground. Shaking, she forced herself to her feet.

> *"Leave this place.*
>
> *"Leave this ...*
>
> *"Leave ...*
>
> *"Le ..."*

The words disintegrated, breaking up into fragments of sentences, scraps of meaning, and then the sounds themselves dissolved into an indistinguishable guttural mumbling.

With her eyes fixed firmly on the light-box, Claire bent her head and ran blindly through the narrow tunnel, banging off the walls, grazing her hands and knees, cracking her elbow off the stones, before she stumbled out into the cold morning air where she threw herself on the ground, her heart thumping, her chest heaving. She was surprised to find tears in her eyes; she hadn't realised she'd been crying.

Coming to her knees, she pressed the heels of both hands into her eyes and angrily brushed the tears away – she wasn't going to let Patrick see her crying. Just because that place had got to her and she'd panicked ...

When she took her hands away from her face, she saw a figure standing across the field watching her.

Claire raised an arm and waved. "Hello ... hello? I need some help ..." Her voice sounded high-pitched and shaky.

It was a man, though it was almost impossible to make out any details because the rising sun was burning the dew off the grass and a white mist was coiling up around him like smoke. He was wearing a battered hat that threw his eyes and most of his face into shadow. "Hello ..." Claire tried again.

The mist swirled and billowed, blanketing the figure, and when it blew away, he had vanished.

The girl wrapped her arms across her chest. She felt very alone, and very afraid.

Chapter Five

Police sirens wailed across the frosty Irish countryside, bringing Claire to her feet. Shading her eyes she looked down at the road where flashing blue lights bounced off the hedges. A blue police car slid into the empty car park, tyres screaming. As soon as the car stopped, Patrick jumped out and ran towards her, slipping and skidding on the damp grass. "Claire!" He caught her in his arms and hugged her tightly. "Are you all right?"

"I had to get out ..." she began in a rush. "The torch died and I heard voices, whispers ..." But she stopped as three ambulances, two more police cars and a fire engine arrived, all with their sirens blaring. More sirens warbled in the distance. The two teenagers were brushed aside as the police, fire-brigade and ambulance crews hurried into the mound. Patrick and Claire stood in silence and watched the first bodies being carried out, the stretcher-bearers struggling awkwardly through the narrow entranceway.

Patrick put his arm around Claire's shoulder and led her away from the mound. A small crowd of curious onlookers had gathered now, and a television crew was setting up, a young reporter with a microphone taking up position so that the mound would be behind him when he spoke into the camera.

"We'd better keep away from them," Patrick said. "We don't want them asking awkward questions – at least, not until we've got our story straight."

Claire broke in abruptly. "There he is again."

"Who?"

The girl pointed to one side, away from the crowd.

Patrick squinted short-sightedly. "The old tramp?"

"I saw him earlier when I came out of the mound. I called to him for help, but he walked away and ignored me."

"Probably didn't want to get involved," Patrick said. He watched as the tramp disappeared into the crowd. "Anyway, you didn't get around to telling me what happened. You said you heard voices?" He was unable to keep the tone of disbelief from his voice.

"I *thought* I heard voices," Claire quickly corrected him. Standing out here in the early-morning sunshine, it sounded so ridiculous. She shrugged. "I suppose I just got a bit scared. I was sitting in the middle of a prehistoric mound, surrounded by unconscious bodies, and my torch suddenly went out. That's when I thought I heard voices ..."

"Voices?"

"Noises. I heard noises. But they sounded like voices," she added. She stopped and thought about the sounds, shuddering with the memory. "Like someone laughing."

"It was just your imagination," Patrick said gently.

"I know," Claire nodded. "But they sounded so real."

Patrick waved an arm around. "Sounds carry on the air," he said. "And I suppose they could be funnelled in through the opening and bounced off the stones. You might have been hearing someone talking on the other side of the fields."

"I know. I thought that too. But it seemed as if the sounds were coming from inside the mound," Claire said softly.

They were heading back to the police car when the reporter appeared before them, microphone held in front of him like a stick. "Hi. I'm Mark Kelly, Nine O'Clock News. Did you belong to the group that had the accident?" Before they had a chance to answer, he had manoeuvred them around so that they were facing the cameraman with the camera perched on his shoulder. Lights came on, blinding them both. "Now, just be natural and answer my questions. Talk to me, and don't look at the camera."

"We've nothing to say," Patrick said.

The reporter ignored them. Turning back to face the camera, he raised the microphone. "I am now talking to two survivors of the mystery illness that has struck down an entire classroom and their teacher ..." When he turned back to Patrick and Claire, he discovered that they had walked away. "Hey," he shouted. "Come back. I want to talk to you."

Patrick drew Claire closer. "We don't want to talk to you," he yelled.

"You'll be on television," the reporter began, but the teenagers stopped beside a police car and a large red-cheeked sergeant raised his head and turned to glare at the reporter. As Patrick followed Claire into the back of the police car, the young man grinned cheekily at the reporter.

"You're perfectly healthy," the doctor said, quickly scribbling a note on a yellow pad.

Patrick was buttoning up his shirt. "How is everyone else?"

The doctor was a small hard-faced man, with permanent wrinkles etched into his forehead. "They're fine," he said quickly. "All sleeping comfortably now. There are a few abrasions and contusions, and one young woman has a fractured wrist, but there's nothing more serious than that. We've run every test we know on them, but they all came up negative." He shrugged. "We'll keep them in for observation and, unless there are any complications overnight, we'll let them go in the morning."

"So everyone's okay, then?" Patrick breathed a sigh of relief.

The ambulances had taken the unconscious students and teacher to Our Lady of Lourdes Hospital in Drogheda, the nearest hospital to Newgrange. The convoy of ambulances and police cars roared through the quiet country roads, while police motor-cycle outriders cleared the way. It was thrilling – and for a few brief moments, Patrick found himself enjoying the experience. Then, when he remembered that they were following their schoolfriends, lying still and unconscious in the back of the ambulances, he felt guilty.

It was chaos at the hospital. The press had got hold of the story and the ambulance bays were filled with photographers and news crews. The police were trying to hold them back, but they surged forward when the first ambulance swerved into the bay and the back doors swung open. Dozens of flashguns lit up each stretcher as it was taken out of the back of the ambulance, and when the police sergeant – Sergeant Doolin, he'd said his name was – led Claire and Patrick into the hospital, the press shouted questions after them.

"What was it like ..."

"What happened ..."

"Why weren't you affected ..."

"Are there any fatalities ..."

"... give us a comment ..."

The sergeant had put his big hands on their shoulders, pushing them forward, protecting them with his bulk. "Ignore them," he said shortly. "Don't even look at them."

Patrick and Claire were separated in the hospital and they both underwent a battery of tests – blood, urine, sputum, then X-rays and breathing exercises.

It was close to three o'clock in the afternoon before the doctors finally pronounced them fit and well. Patrick was exhausted – he'd been up since five o'clock that morning – and he knew that Claire would be feeling much the same.

The doctor added another cryptic note on the yellow pad.

"We thought there might have been gas in the chamber," Patrick said, tucking his shirt into his jeans.

The doctor nodded absently. "That seems logical, but there is no evidence of gas inhalation ..." he began, and then abruptly remembered that he was speaking to someone he considered little more than a child. "Everyone is fine," he repeated.

"Then what knocked them out?" the young man insisted.

The doctor closed the folder with a snap and frowned at Patrick. "We don't know," he said eventually. "Hysteria, possibly."

"Hysteria?" Patrick said incredulously. "*Hysteria?*"

The creases on the doctor's forehead deepened to straight lines. "Someone probably fainted – a combination of the dark and maybe lack of sleep and a poor breakfast. The other people in the chamber got a fright, they panicked, then one by one, they fainted too."

Patrick was about to reply, then bit his lip and said nothing. He realised that the doctor didn't know what had knocked out the entire class, and was simply giving him a lame excuse. He too had had little sleep, and no breakfast, other than a cup of tea – and he hadn't fainted. No; something had happened inside the mound, his classmates had seen or experienced something ... something strange. He'd have to wait until he got the chance to talk to some of his friends.

"When can I go home?" he asked.

The doctor shrugged. "Whenever you wish. I understand the principal of your school is here. She has come to collect you and Miss ... Miss ..." he couldn't remember Claire's name and Patrick deliberately didn't tell him. "You and the young woman who came in with you," he finished in a rush. "If you experience any discomfort over the next few days – headaches, difficulty in breathing, palpitations, problems with sleeping – then contact your local doctor. It'll be just a nervous reaction to today's events and nothing to worry about."

He ushered Patrick towards the door and pulled it open.

There was a uniformed police officer sitting on a chair in the corridor. He stood up when the door opened. "You can take this young man to ... to ..." The doctor paused. He didn't know where Patrick was supposed to go.

"Yes, sir." The police officer saluted. He put his hand on Patrick's shoulder and turned him down the corridor. "And how are you?" he asked when the door closed.

"I'm fine," Patrick repeated for the hundredth time. From the moment he had set foot inside the hospital, people had been asking him how he was. "Have you any idea what happened?" he asked, glancing sidelong at the officer.

"Gas," the young officer said. "It probably built up in the chamber overnight; your group were first in there this morning, and it knocked them out."

Patrick nodded quickly. He had been thinking exactly the same thing.

The officer looked at Patrick. "I still can't figure out why you and Miss Holland weren't affected."

"We had stepped outside for a breath of air," Patrick said quickly.

They turned right at the bottom of the corridor and stopped outside a door marked Matron's Office. The police officer tapped on the door and turned the handle. When Patrick entered the room and saw Claire sitting on a high-backed wooden chair facing him, he felt a surge of relief wash over him. But when the door closed, he noticed the stick-thin figure of the school headmistress, Mrs Keogh, who was rising to her feet.

"Patrick Elliot. And how are you? This is a terrible business," she said, before he had time to answer, "a terrible business." She stared hard at him over the rims of her half-glasses, almost as if she thought he was responsible. "How are you?" she repeated.

"Fine, Miss," he said tiredly.

"I'm taking you both home. In the circumstances, you can have the rest of the day off ... but I will expect to see you in school tomorrow."

"Yes, Miss," they both chorused.

Chapter Six

I t tested its bonds ... and found that they had weakened.

Soon it would be free.

Warm sun and cold stone, old magic and white light had bound it here for countless generations – aware, awake, unsleeping, undying.

At mid-winter, when the year hung in the balance, when the old year had died and the new had not yet begun, the spell weakened ... until the pure shafting light of the new sun washed across the blessed stones and rekindled the primeval spell. Then the cold magic blazed afresh, burning its body with icy fire. It writhed in agony and its howling troubled the sleep of those who lived closest to the House of the Dead, bringing nightmares and dread thoughts.

And there were times when it thought that it would never be free, that it was condemned to spend all eternity beneath the ancient mound.

Until now.

This year the first shaft of light had not touched the stones.

It tested its bonds again, twisting, turning, loosening packed earth and old magic, crushing ancient stones and rotten wood. Clawing upwards.

Soon it would be free.

Soon.

Chapter Seven

Still damp from her long hot bath, Claire slid between the warm sheets, pulled them up to her chin and watched with sleepy eyes while her mother fussed around the room. "We were so worried," the white-haired woman kept repeating, "so worried."

"I'm fine, Mum," Claire muttered. Now that she was finally in bed, she felt exhaustion wash over her like a leaden weight. Her eyes felt gritty with tiredness, there was a dull throbbing at the back of her head, and she could still smell the sharp medicinal odour of the hospital in her nostrils.

"When I heard it on the news," Moira Holland continued, "I didn't know what to think. And of course when I phoned the school looking for the headmistress, I was told that she was unavailable." She picked up Claire's navy blue school jumpers and pushed them into a drawer. "I was frantic with worry. I'm going to complain to the school first thing in the morning." The small sharp-faced woman folded her arms and stood at the bottom of the bed. "You should never have been taken to Newgrange in the first place. I think it was absolutely disgraceful and irresponsible to bring people out to the middle of nowhere at dawn in December ..."

"Mother," Claire said forcefully, "what happened was an accident. Nothing more. Just a freakish accident. And everyone is all right, nothing more serious than a few cuts and bruises. And Patrick and I weren't even involved ..."

"I don't know what your father is going to say about it when he comes home from work."

"Oh, Mum," Claire said tiredly. She closed her eyes and breathed deeply, blocking out her mother's monotonous droning. Gradually, her breathing deepened into an easy rhythm. When Moira Holland realised that her daughter was asleep, she moved around the bed, tucking her in, then tiptoed from the room.

As soon as Claire heard the bedroom door click shut she opened her eyes again and pushed herself up in the bed. A cup of sweet tepid tea sat on her bedside locker. Wrapping both hands around it, she sipped slowly, grimacing at the sickly-sweet taste. She usually took one spoonful of sugar in her tea, but she guessed that her mother – who knew that sugar was supposed to be good for shock – had laced this cup with half-a-dozen heaped teaspoonfuls. Resting her head back against the pink padded headboard, she tried to make sense of everything that had happened. But, no matter how hard she tried, she still couldn't explain exactly what had taken place in the mound. Had she really heard voices, or was that nothing more than her imagination? When she heard them first, they sounded so real, but they were beginning to fade now, taking on the texture of an old dream. She tried to recall exactly what she'd heard, but she couldn't even remember the words, only the overall tone of ... of triumph ... of victory. As she returned her teacup to the bedside locker, she noticed the time on her clock-radio: six-thirty.

Twelve hours.

She had actually left the house at six-thirty this morning in order to be down at the school by seven. The minibus left at seven-fifteen and Miss Lee had promised that they would wait for no-one.

Patrick had been waiting for her at the bus-stop at the end of the road. She was surprised to find him there; usually she was the one who had to wait. They had walked the quarter mile to the school in an easy silence, not speaking, enjoying the unusual experience of being out so early. The morning was bitterly cold, the night stars still sparkled sharply overhead, and the footpath glistened with frost. Patrick skidded once, grabbing Claire's arm for support, almost pulling her down with him. Their laughter sounded like broken glass on the icy air.

Claire had known Patrick all her life. They had grown up together in a small suburban estate on the north side of Dublin that was gradually being swallowed up into the encroaching city. Neither had brothers or sisters, and their parents were close friends, so it was natural that the children should play together. They went through primary school together, always in the same class and ended up in the same class in secondary school. They were both intelligent, easily bored in class and shared a mischievous sense of humour that more than once had landed them in hot water. Whenever there was trouble at school, it could usually be traced back to either Claire or Patrick – or both.

Patrick wasn't her boyfriend – Claire felt herself smile at the very idea – and she was definitely not his girlfriend. But when people saw them together, they always seemed to come to that conclusion and, somehow, Patrick never seemed to go out with any other girls, and although she occasionally danced with other boys at the Friday night discos, she always walked home with Patrick. She was fond of him, and his concern for her today had touched her, but when she thought of him, she always considered him the brother she never had. There were times when she wondered if their relationship would ever change. She would be sixteen next birthday – and so would Patrick – and she supposed things would have to change, though she wasn't sure if she wanted that.

She heard the front door opening below, and glanced at the clock again. Six-fifty. That would be her father coming home from work. She listened intently, filtering out the sounds of the TV drifting up from the sitting room. She snuggled back beneath the covers when she heard the stairs creak.

The door opened a crack, a sliver of white light splitting the room in two. "Are you asleep?"

"Dad?" she said softly, when she realised he was alone. She could hear her mother moving about in the kitchen.

Chris Holland stepped into the room, leaving the door ajar to provide light. "How are you?" He sat on the edge of the bed and took his daughter's hands in his. His skin was rough, gritty with cement and dirt. "Your mother told me what happened. Are you all right?"

"I'm fine, Dad, honestly. I'm fine. I wasn't even in the mound when the others were gassed."

"Your mother said you were taken to hospital," her father said in his slow deliberate fashion.

"We were all taken to hospital. Everyone was unconscious, except for Patrick and myself ..."

"I was wondering where he came into all this," Chris Holland said with a grin, his teeth flashing whitely in the gloom. "Tell me, how did the pair of you manage to escape?"

Claire was glad that there was only the tiny crack of light in the room. Her father claimed that he could tell by looking into her eyes if she was lying. So far he had never been proven wrong. "We were the last of the group to go into the mound," she said truthfully. "We came back out because it was dark and stuffy in the tunnel that led into the central chamber," she added. "And you know what Patrick's claustrophobia is like," she said quickly, making a mental note to tell Patrick that he now suffered from claustrophobia.

Her father nodded. He was quite sure he wasn't getting the full story here, and he had his own ideas why Claire and Patrick had slipped out. He was only too aware of the reputation they both had at school; they'd probably intended to let down the tyres of the minibus. "What happened in the hospital?" he asked.

Claire squirmed uncomfortably. "I didn't know there were so many samples that could be taken from you," she said. "But both Patrick and I came up with a clean bill of health. We were allowed to go home, though the hospital said it would keep Miss Lee and the rest of the class in for observation."

"Probably let them home tomorrow," Chris said.

"That's what the doctor said."

Her father stood up, the mattress creaking. "See – I knew that. I could have been a doctor."

"You should have been, Dad."

"There's more money in building houses," Chris grinned. Leaning forward, he kissed his daughter on the forehead. "Get some rest now; it's been an exhausting day for you. Come down later on and you can have something to eat."

Claire nodded. "I should phone Patrick," she said suddenly. "Just a quick call to make sure he's all right."

"Use the phone in the bedroom, and don't let your mother know you're awake," her father said with a smile.

Claire waited until her father had gone into the bathroom and she heard the taps running before she hopped out of bed and tiptoed into her parents' bedroom. Sitting on the edge of the hideous multicoloured quilt her mother had spent an entire winter making, she lifted the portable phone from its cradle and extended the aerial. Before dialling the seven digits she pressed the phone to her ear to make sure she had a line.

Static crackled and buzzed, dissolved, sparked, crackled again ... forming words.

"Watching ...

"Waiting ...

"Wait ...

"Come ...

"Coming ..."

The phone slid from Claire's numb fingers and bounced

43

on to the bed. A cold sick feeling twisted in the pit of her stomach. It was the voice ... the voice from the mound.

Chapter Eight

"Quick, Patrick, this is the bit." Dave Elliot pointed the remote control at the television and stabbed the volume button. The sound swelled suddenly, deafeningly, and he quickly lowered it again.

Patrick came in from the kitchen and perched on the edge of the settee beside his mother and father to watch the item on the Nine O'Clock News. His parents already knew it by heart from the early news broadcast, but Patrick hadn't seen it yet. It gave him a peculiar feeling to see Newgrange on TV where, only a few hours earlier, he had actually been standing on that stone – just above the door. A long line of stretchers was being carried from the mound.

"... *mysterious illness that struck down an entire class* ..."

The scene shifted to the hospital, showing the ambulances arriving.

"*The injured were treated at Our Lady of Lourdes Hospital* ..."

Dave Elliot nudged his son with his elbow. "Any second now ..."

"Two students unaffected by the illness reported a mysterious smell ..."

It took Patrick a few seconds to realise that the two small, pale-faced teenagers being led from a police car into the hospital were Claire and himself. He squirmed in embarrassment: did he really look like that? His hair was sticking up at the back, his glasses tilted crookedly on his face, and he thought his eyes looked really wild and scared. Claire looked better than he did, almost exactly the way she always looked, except that her cheeks were bright red.

"I look awful," he said, horrified.

"No you don't," his mother said absently.

"Doctors are baffled. There is speculation that there may have been a build-up of toxic gasses inside the mound overnight. Newgrange will remain closed to the public until the incident has been investigated. This is Mark Kelly, reporting for ..."

"I saw him this morning," Patrick said, suddenly recognising the young reporter. "He tried to get an interview with Claire and me."

"Why didn't you agree? You'd have been on TV – a celebrity!" Dave Elliot grinned. He raised the remote control and snapped the TV off as the newscaster moved on to the next item. "You sure you're feeling okay?" he asked, looking at his son, his voice low and serious.

"I'm fine, Da. Honestly. Just a little tired. But that's probably because I was up at six this morning."

Joyce Elliot peered over her clicking knitting needles. "You should get an early night, Patrick. You do look tired."

Patrick started to shake his head, but his father said firmly,

"Your mother's right, son. You look exhausted and you've got black bags the size of suitcases under your eyes. Why don't you head on up to bed now. You could do with the extra couple of hours, otherwise you might be sick over Christmas – and you don't want that to happen, now do you?"

"No, Da." Patrick got slowly to his feet. He really was feeling tired, and every muscle and joint in his body ached. He'd thought about running a bath earlier, but he knew he hadn't the energy. He'd probably fall asleep and wake up sitting in icy water with his skin looking like wrinkled cloth. "You're right. I'll go now. Goodnight," he muttered.

"I'll bring you up a cup of tea later if you're still awake," his mother called after him.

Patrick climbed the stairs, yawning hugely, feeling his jaw muscles pop with the effort. He had meant to phone Claire earlier, but he just hadn't got around to it, and if she was as tired as he was, she was probably in bed by now. He'd see her at school tomorrow.

Patrick flopped down on his bed with his hands behind his head and stared at the ceiling. His model aeroplanes, suspended on lengths of nearly invisible fishing line, swung silently, twisting to and fro in a breeze he couldn't feel.

What a day!

Patrick kicked his shoes off, allowing them to thump on to the floor.

He wondered what had really happened inside New-grange. Was it toxic gas or hysteria? Or had someone fainted, and the rest of the class followed suit? But that was just too difficult to believe. He couldn't see someone like Tommy

Butler fainting! Tommy was his best friend and wasn't afraid of anything. Patrick's thin lips twisted into a quick smile: he had a sudden image of the class falling down like dominoes, one after the other. The smile faded when he remembered seeing the bodies lying still and unmoving on the ground.

The best part of the day had been driving the school minibus. He hadn't been entirely truthful when he'd told Claire that he could drive. His Dad had given him a few lessons, so he knew the basics, but there was a big difference between driving an eight-year-old Toyota in the local car park and a three-year-old sixteen-seater minibus along narrow and icy country roads. He crashed the gears a dozen times before he finally managed to get the hang of it, almost drove it off the road twice – once on a corner when he hit a patch of ice – and he was pulling up outside the police station when he had backed into a lamp-post, shattering one of the rear indicator lights.

With an effort, Patrick sat up on the bed, pulled off his jumper and began to unbutton his shirt.

Driving the van had been the easy part though, he had to admit that ... at least he had been moving away from Newgrange. There was no way he could have stayed behind to stand guard over the sleeping bodies. No way! It reminded him of too many scenes from late-night horror movies – he would have been expecting them to rise up like broken puppets and chase him out of the mound. But Claire didn't watch that type of movie.

Patrick stopped.

Why was Claire outside the mound when he returned with the police? She told him about the voices, but he hadn't had time to quiz her further. Events had moved so quickly. They rode to the hospital in the police car, in the hospital they'd been separated, and on the way back to Dublin in Mrs Keogh's car neither of them had felt inclined to talk. Indeed, most of the trip had been conducted in stony silence, with Mrs Keogh radiating anger and annoyance. Aside from being worried and upset about her teacher and students, the headmistress was most annoyed that her school had been brought into the limelight in this way. And although she had said nothing, she made it perfectly clear that she held Patrick and Claire somehow responsible for what had happened.

Patrick reached beneath his pillow and pulled out his pyjamas. He glanced at the clock-radio as he climbed into bed: it was half-past nine. He couldn't remember the last time he had been in bed by nine-thirty, especially in Christmas week.

Christmas.

Only three days to Christmas. It wasn't going to be much of a Christmas this year. His father or mother hadn't worked for more than two years and although his parents had said nothing to him, he knew money was very tight. He was aware that his mother was buying less and less food every week, concentrating only on necessities. They hadn't asked what he wanted for Christmas this year, nor had he made any requests. He'd got presents for his parents with money saved from the meagre wages from his paper round – a cardigan for his mother, a classical CD for his father – but he hadn't got anything for Claire yet. He'd have to take care of that Thursday evening or maybe Friday, Christmas Eve.

Rolling over in the bed, Patrick thumbed on the radio.

He was thinking about getting her the latest Julian Lennon album on cassette, and he'd seen a great Baywatch poster that he knew she'd love.

The radio hissed with static. Patrick frowned. It should have been tuned to 98FM. He moved the tuning wheel, watching the red line on the dial inch forward. He caught the ghost of music, something harsh and discordant, and continued tuning. A foreign-sounding voice appeared and disappeared. Who had been messing with his radio? Static crackled again, suddenly forming words ...

> *"Watching ...*
>
> *"Waiting ...*
>
> *"Wait ...*
>
> *"Come ...*
>
> *"Coming ..."*

Raucous pop music abruptly replaced the harsh whispers. Patrick snapped off the sound with trembling fingers. Watching, waiting, coming? It was just interference or a foreign channel, maybe a BBC play, nothing more. But why did the words seem so terrifying? Watching. Waiting. Coming?

What was watching ... what was waiting ... what was coming?

Patrick lay back on the pillow, suddenly reluctant to turn out the light.

Chapter Nine

Nurse Aisling Miller moved along the rows of beds, checking on the sleeping patients. These were the students who had collapsed in Newgrange this morning. The seven males were in this ward, while the five female students and their teacher were in the next. The young nurse had heard about the accident on the news before she came on duty, and although she knew they had been taken to the hospital in Drogheda, she never thought she would be caring for them. The hospital was buzzing with speculation and rumour. There were news vans in the car park outside and reporters prowling the corridors, looking for someone to interview – hoping above all to get a comment from one of the students. She was one of the few people who knew that the reporters were wasting their time; no-one was going to tell them anything – simply because there was nothing to tell.

No-one actually knew what had happened to the group. The medical examinations hadn't shown up anything and they were all in good health except for some cuts and bruises which they'd acquired when they'd fallen. The press were speculating about a build-up of gas in the mound, but tests on the students' lung linings, throats and nasal passages had revealed no signs of toxic gas inhalation.

Aisling Miller had discovered that there had been some concern in the hospital when none of the thirteen patients showed any signs of regaining consciousness as the day progressed. Ambulances had actually started to arrive to ferry them down to one of the bigger hospitals in Dublin for further tests and brain scans when, late in the afternoon, the students had begun waking up one by one. Miss Lee, their teacher, was the last to awaken. They had all been terribly confused and some of them were frightened. One girl kept asking if this was a dream, and saying that she wanted to wake up. Although they had parents and friends around to comfort them, the nurse noticed that one doctor had written in his report that the patients had seemed distant and with-drawn, almost as if they were unaware of their surroundings. Under questioning, no-one remembered what had hap-pened in the mound. Their last conscious memory was of standing in the heart of Newgrange waiting for the sun to come shining in through the light-box.

Hysteria, Aisling Miller concluded. Mass hysteria.

Starting with the last bed on the left-hand side of the ward, Nurse Miller lifted the chart, tilting it to the dull light to read the name.

Martin Simms. Male. Fifteen years, three months. He had sustained a cut lip and a bruise to his chin when he'd fallen. The nurse noted that his eyes had been examined by a specialist because the lens in the boy's glasses had shattered in the fall. They were checking just in case there were slivers in his eye, but no foreign bodies had been discovered.

Working quickly and efficiently, the nurse took blood pressure – normal – and temperature, a little high, but that was to be expected. Under 'Comments' she wrote that the patient was sleeping easily, then she moved on to the next bed.

Thomas Butler. Male. Fifteen years, six months. He too was uninjured except for extensive bruising down the left-hand side of his body where he'd obviously struck the stone wall when he'd fallen.

Aisling Miller was bending down to take the boy's temperature when she heard the sound. She straightened, listening intently, blanking out the normal hospital night-time sounds, concentrating on the noise. It sounded like whispering. Urgent whispering.

Someone calling her? A patient in distress?

Nurse Miller walked down the centre of the ward, moving silently on rubber-soled shoes. She nodded unconsciously: it was whispering. She could almost make out the words.

"Watch ..."

She stopped at the nurses' station at the bottom of the ward, checking to make sure that the intercom wasn't on, or that one of the other nurses hadn't left a radio playing.

"Wait ..."

She walked into the next ward, where the female patients lay. Nurse Redmond was at the end of the ward making notes on a clipboard.

"Rose," Aisling Miller said softly, "were you calling me?"

"Come ..."

The older nurse shook her head. "Not me."

"I thought I heard someone whispering."

"Maybe one of the patients talking in their sleep?" the older nurse suggested. "It happens all the time, you'll get used it."

"Don't you hear anything?"

The nurse stood still, her head tilted back. "Nothing," she said eventually.

The young nurse walked back into the male ward, moving slowly from bed to bed. None of the patients was talking in his sleep, though she still kept hearing the fragments of hissing whispers. She noticed that all the young men's eyes were darting behind their closed lids. They were all dreaming. And then she realised that they were all twitching, moving uneasily in the beds, as if they were disturbed by their dreams.

The nurse shivered though the ward was warm. She wondered what they were dreaming about.

"Come ...

"Coming ..."

On impulse, she wandered back into the female ward. She was not surprised to discover that they too were dreaming, their eyes darting wildly, their limbs twitching.

The whispers intensified.

"Coming ...

"Coming ...

"Coming ..."

The young nurse tried to convince herself that it was gas escaping from one of the oxygen tanks at the end of the hall ... but she knew she wasn't hearing the hiss of escaping gas.

Chapter Ten

Patrick dreamed.
Weight.

Solid, heavy weight pressing down on his arms and legs, squeezing the air from his lungs.

Weight.

He was deep underground, his hands stretched up over his head supporting the roof of a tunnel that was threatening to cave in at any moment. Tendrils of dirt and earth slipped out from beneath his fingers and trickled on to his face, into his eyes and nose and mouth.

Far, far above him, he could hear the faint sounds of people moving about, laughing softly, voices raised in questions. He tried to call out to them, but there was earth in his mouth, and he hadn't got the strength to draw the breath into his lungs to shout.

But now he could feel the additional weight of the people above. Sections of the roof were crumbling away as they tramped around. The entire ceiling shifted, the cold damp earth pressing down on him, driving him to his knees, while he still tried to keep the roof above his head.

And he knew he had to keep the roof up because someone was trapped deeper in the tunnel.

Someone?

Claire!

Claire was trapped further down the tunnel. He knew that right now she was crawling up this way, and he had to keep the passage open for her. But the weight, the terrible oppressive weight was driving him down, the effort tearing at his shoulders, elbows and wrists, wrapping an iron band around his chest. He couldn't breathe, couldn't move. He was trapped. The tunnel was collapsing in around him and he was trapped, buried alive underground, and he would remain here for all eternity.

He opened his mouth to scream, but it filled with cold, damp earth ...

Patrick awoke with a shout, fighting his way out from beneath the blankets that he had become entangled in. He pulled the edge of the pillowcase out of his mouth. He was drenched with sweat, shaking with reaction: the dream had been so vivid. He turned the clock to check the time. It was three-ten in the morning, and he knew he wasn't going to sleep again this night.

Claire dreamed.

Cold.

Numbing, bitter cold, turning her arms and legs to blocks of brittle ice, every breath in her lungs so frigid it burned. She knew she was trapped in a cave deep underground, in a place without light or heat, a place where the sun never shone, a place of perpetual cold and dark, where sleek creatures with razor-sharp teeth and no legs slithered and coiled, where blind, hairless rodents skittered in the corners.

Although every movement was an effort, Claire knew that she had to get out. Escape lay down this corridor. She knew it led towards the light. But the roof of the tunnel was crumbling away, stone and earth crashing down, blocking the exit. If only she could get into the tunnel and feel the sun on her flesh, she would be warm again.

She reached for the tunnel opening, but her hand was encased in a block of ice. It shattered when she touched the wall, and she could move her fingers, but even as she watched, the rime formed over her hands again, turning the pale flesh blue, her fingernails curling into black stubs.

She opened her mouth to scream, but it filled with bitter liquid, which hardened to solid ice, encasing her teeth and tongue. Her tears were crystals of ice which hardened on her cheeks.

Claire awoke, shivering uncontrollably. She had kicked off the heavy duvet and the central heating had obviously switched itself off. The room was so cold she could actually see her breath pluming whitely in the air before her. Dragging the duvet off the floor, she wrapped it around her body and propped herself up against the pink headboard. She glanced at the clock – it was ten past three in the morning – she didn't think she was going to sleep again this night.

Chapter Eleven

Mrs Keogh looked up from the report on her desk. Adjusting her glasses, she thrust her head forward and squinted over the top of the half-frames at the two students standing before her. "I find it extraordinary," she began, "that whenever there is any trouble in this school, whenever something goes wrong, or something doesn't work, I always seem to find that the names of Patrick Elliot and Claire Holland are mentioned." She paused, almost as if she was expecting one or other of them to reply. "So it comes as little surprise to find that you were on the ill-fated field-trip to Newgrange yesterday, and you will excuse me if I find it curious that the only two students unaffected by this extraordinary affair are both of you."

Neither Patrick nor Claire said anything. This wasn't the first time they had stood in the headmistress's office, and they knew better than to answer her back.

Mrs Keogh had two brown files on the desk in front of her. Placing a hand flat on each file, she looked up at Patrick and Claire. "You are both excellent students, though all of your teachers feel that you are not achieving your full potential. I can see no reason why either of you should be so disruptive or downright mischievous in class. Your teachers put it down to boredom."

Patrick frowned. "With respect, Miss. I'm not sure what this has to do with what happened yesterday. It's almost as if you are accusing us of causing the accident."

"We've already told you why we were outside ..." Claire added.

"My claustrophobia," Patrick said, biting the inside of his cheek to prevent himself from smiling. He saw the sudden tightening of Claire's jaw muscles and knew she was trying her hardest not to laugh too. He thought the claustrophobia story was a master-stroke.

"This is the first time we've learned about your claustrophobia," Mrs Keogh said icily.

"It was the first time we were in Newgrange, Miss," Patrick said quickly.

"Your claustrophobia didn't manifest itself when you crawled along inside the air vents to deliver a live mouse into Miss Anderson's chemistry class, did it?"

"No, Miss," Patrick muttered.

"So you will understand if I take this sudden occurrence of claustrophobia with a large grain of salt."

"No, Miss. I mean, yes, Miss."

"Is there anything you would like to tell me now?" the headmistress asked.

"About what?" Claire asked innocently.

"About what happened yesterday morning," Mrs Keogh said evenly.

"We've told you what happened," Claire said smoothly.

The headmistress laced her fingers together and stared hard at the girl, before turning her head slightly to look at the boy. She had been a teacher for more than thirty years. She had taught thousands of children, from junior infants right up to teenagers. She knew when she was being lied to. And she knew she was being lied to now.

Initially, she suspected that either Patrick or Claire – probably Patrick who excelled at chemistry – had released some sort of gas into the chamber in Newgrange. But the hospital had confirmed that they had found no evidence of gassing. However, when she'd spoken to Miss Lee in the hospital last night, the young history teacher had been muttering about whispers, terrifying whispers that had echoed around the chamber. Probably Patrick, the headmistress concluded. If she could find the evidence that he had caused the outbreak of nervous hysteria, she would expel him – and the girl too.

"So, you have nothing further to add?"

"No, Miss," they said together.

Mrs Keogh nodded. She was a patient woman, and she knew the truth would out – eventually.

"Before you go," she said finally, speaking the words reluctantly, "you should know that a Sergeant Doolin phoned here this morning and congratulated me on your behaviour and quick thinking yesterday." She smiled a thin wintry smile. "I feel I must add my own congratulations to his. I realise that it took an extraordinary amount of courage to go back into the mound when you knew something had happened." She looked at Claire. "I understand that you remained with the injured and tried to make them comfort-able."

Claire nodded.

Mrs Keogh turned to Patrick. "I believe you drove the school bus to the station to alert the police. It was an incredibly risky thing to do, given the icy state of the roads."

"I'm sorry about the light," Patrick said quietly.

Mrs Keogh's thin eyebrows arched. "What light?"

Patrick could have kicked himself. She hadn't noticed the broken light. "I'm afraid I hit a lamp-post and broke an indicator light."

The headmistress attempted a smile, which failed. "Well, in the circumstances, I think we can forgive that. Now, before I let you go to class, I would just like to advise you that I don't think you should give any interviews to the press. We wouldn't want the good name of the school brought into disrepute, would we?"

"No, Miss," they both chorused. "We didn't give any interviews yesterday," Patrick added.

"I think you did the right thing." The headmistress glanced up at the clock on the wall. "You'd better hurry along to your class. You can join Mr O'Brien's maths class, Room 24. He's expecting you."

"Yes, Miss."

"And Claire, Patrick." They turned at the door to look at her. "If you do decide that you want to talk, you know where to find me."

"Yes, Miss. Thank you, Miss."

Patrick breathed a sigh of relief as they walked away from the headmistress's office, their footsteps echoing along the empty corridor. "I know we've done nothing – but I still feel guilty!" He glanced quickly at Claire. "I mean, we haven't done anything wrong, have we?"

She shook her head. "Not as far as I know. Though we did block up the light-box."

"I know. But that couldn't have been responsible for what happened, could it?" he asked.

"I don't think so," Claire said slowly. "Unless people got a fright when the sun didn't come shining in through the hole, and they fainted," she suggested.

Patrick looked sceptical. "Can you see someone like Tommy Butler or Jimmy Molloy getting a fright just because it was *dark*?"

The girl laughed. "You're right. It's probably just coincidence."

"Probably."

Taking advantage of every second out of class, they slowed as they neared the classroom.

"I meant to phone you last night," Patrick said, "but I was too tired. Sorry."

"I went to bed early myself," Claire said. "Not that I got much sleep," she added.

"No. Nor I," Patrick admitted. "Bad dreams," he said with a shaky laugh.

Claire stopped and looked at him. "Bad dreams? So had I."

Patrick turned to look at her. He shrugged his shoulders. "Hardly surprising, considering what happened yesterday."

"I suppose so," Claire sighed. "I dreamt I was trapped underground ..." She stopped, seeing the expression on Patrick's face.

"Was there a tunnel in this dream?" Patrick whispered.

Claire nodded wordlessly.

"And were you trying to make your way out of the tunnel?"

She nodded again.

"And ..."

Pale morning sunlight suddenly sliced out into the shadowy corridor as a door was pulled open. "What do you two think you're doing dawdling in the corridor?" Mr O'Brien's voice boomed off the walls, his enormous bulk filling the classroom doorway.

"We were just coming, sir," Patrick said quickly. "We'll talk later, during the break," he added in a whisper.

"No whispering! And hurry up!" Mr O'Brien snapped.

"Yes, sir," they said together.

"Later," Claire mouthed. "We'll talk later."

Chapter Twelve

The lunchtime bell was still ringing when the first of the children spilled out into the schoolyard in an explosion of sound: screaming, shouting, laughing and cheering. Over the next five minutes the classes gradually emptied for the twenty-minute mid-morning break.

Invisible lines marked out the schoolyard, the older classes moving to the furthest end, nearest the gates, the juniors remaining closest to the school. Within these areas, the groups were broken up into smaller units, with classes sticking together, clusters of friends gathering in tight bunches, boys and girls settling into groups. The juniors tended to run about, playing wild and noisy games, while the majority of the older students, more conscious of their dignity, usually leant with their backs against the walls or huddled together chatting animatedly. During the warmer weather, the older boys would play a ragged game of football on the sports field, but no-one was willing to walk on to the frozen field at this time of year.

The incident at Newgrange was the talk of the school and

Patrick and Claire were immediately surrounded by dozens of people as they came out into the yard, all shouting questions at them at once.

By the time Patrick had managed to satisfy their curiosity and break away from the group around him, Claire had vanished. He wandered off in search of her. But she wasn't with any of her girl friends, and no, they hadn't seen her. Nor was she in her usual place, against the south-facing wall of the bike shed, her face turned to the watery sunlight.

Where was she?

He slipped back into the school and checked the classroom again – although it was forbidden to return to class during break – but she wasn't there either. He knew she hadn't gone home, because her books were still on her desk and her coat was on its hanger beside his in the cloakroom. Becoming anxious, he returned to the schoolyard. Standing on the steps, he rose on his toes and looked out over the milling heads. If she wasn't in the school and she hadn't gone home, then she had to be here. Making an effort to relax, he moved his head slowly from left to right, not consciously looking for anything, simply allowing the images to soak in. He'd used this trick before; sooner or later, his subconscious would recognise something ...

There!

Against the railings, a familiar curl of brown hair, a remembered tilt of the head. It was Claire. But what was she doing standing there, clutching the metal bars and staring out across the road? Patrick craned his neck, trying to see over the heads of the students, wondering what she was looking at so intently. His short-sightedness only allowed him to make out a vague shape standing across the road from her, under the shadow of a bare winter tree.

As he pushed his way through the crowd, making towards her, the bell rang stridently, calling the students back inside. He saw Claire actually jump with fright. When he reached her, the bottom part of the schoolyard was empty, and she was alone, standing against the railings, holding on to the rusted metal bars with a white-knuckled grip.

"Claire? Claire? Are you okay?"

"It's him, Patrick," she said, without turning around.

The boy stepped up beside her and looked out through the bars. The street was deserted except for an old tramp leaning up against the gnarled trunk of a dead tree on the opposite side of the road. His filthy coat and grey skin were exactly the same colour as the bark.

"That's him, Patrick."

"Who?" He squinted at the tramp, but he was standing well back in shadow and it was difficult to make out his features.

"He was at Newgrange yesterday."

Patrick stepped forward, staring hard. "Are you sure?"

"Positive. When I came out of the mound, he was standing on the opposite side of the field, staring at me. I called out to him, asking for help, but he just turned away."

"You're sure you're not mistaken?"

"I'm sure," she snapped.

"Then what's he doing here?" Patrick wondered aloud.

"Watching us," Claire whispered. "Watching us!"

Chapter Thirteen

Although its physical body was still imprisoned, its mind soared free, dancing from each of the twelve male and female children and the adult female it had touched. It found so many memories, so many dreams and desires.

There was so much to learn.

Time.

So much time had passed. The physical world around it had changed, altered beyond all recognition. It had once occupied a world of rich earth and clean air, of sparkling water and fresh fruits. Now much of this world was foul, the rivers and oceans stank, the air was tainted and the soil was barren. It preferred the world as it was now; it was more to its liking.

And the people: so many teeming millions of the human-kind, like the grains of sand on a beach.

Soft-skinned human-kind.

Hunger burned within like a fire.

At first, it thought that the human-kind had also changed. They knew so much, even the children's minds were filled to bursting with strange and bizarre facts. But when it had probed their thoughts and memories, sifted through their dreams, examined their knowledge, it found so much of it useless, impractical, unnecessary.

So, the human-kind hadn't changed at all: they were still as weak-willed as ever, perhaps even more so now, because whereas once they had their religion to turn to, their priests to protect them, these modern people had no gods to call upon, no priests or priestesses to do battle on their behalf.

Wait ...

It had waited for so long, so very long; all it had to do now was to wait a little longer.

Come ...

It was coming ...

Coming.

Soon.

Then it would feed.

Chapter Fourteen

Claire was waiting for Patrick as he came out the school gates. As usual, he was amongst the last of the stragglers.

"Sorry," he apologised, stopping in front of her, "I got held up. O'Brien was giving me hell about the results of the maths test."

Claire nodded. "I know. I saw him talking to you. Don't tell me you failed again?"

Patrick puffed his cheeks out into a passable imitation of Mr O'Brien's face and mimicked his voice. "Another a-*bis*-mal failure, Mr Elliot. Ab-so-lute-ly a-*bis*-mal."

Claire smiled. "And what did you say?"

"I told him I didn't know what a-*bis*-mal meant," he grinned. The smile faded. "So he made me go down to the library, get out the dictionary and look it up, then write out the explanation and take it back down to him in the staff room. It took me ages to find the word. I didn't know there was a 'y' in abysmal."

Shaking her head, Claire picked her schoolbag off the

ground, heaved it on to her shoulder and turned down the road. Patrick fell into step beside her. "I've been thinking about yesterday," she said quietly.

Patrick glanced sidelong at her, but said nothing. In the late afternoon December light, her features were becoming blurred and grainy, like an out-of-focus photograph, but he could tell from her voice that she was preoccupied.

"Do you think ... I mean, is it possible ..." She took a deep breath and tried again. "Is it possible that we were somehow responsible for what happened yesterday?" She turned to him, and her eyes were wide and frightened, looking like black holes against her pale skin.

They walked on in silence, then Patrick finally admitted, "I don't know. I've been thinking about it. I know it's probably nothing more than a coincidence but ..."

"But it's just too much of a coincidence," Claire finished.

The boy nodded unhappily. "It is," he agreed.

They turned left at the bottom of the road, cutting through the building site where a new housing estate was being built. As they walked down what would one day be the main road, they could hear the distant shouts and fading echoing cries of the other students taking the same short-cut – even though the whole construction area was marked clearly with numerous 'PRIVATE – KEEP OUT' signs. Usually this place would be a hive of activity, brilliant arc lights illuminating the site, allowing the workers to continue late into the evenings, but the site was now deserted and in deep shadow. The workers had finished up yesterday for the Christmas holidays.

"I mean, everything was fine until we blocked up the

71

entrance," Claire continued. One of the things Patrick liked about Claire was that she always accepted responsibility for what they'd done together, sharing the blame when it went wrong. Another person might have said: When *you* blocked up the entrance; but not Claire. "I wish we knew exactly what happened inside," she murmured.

Patrick reached out and caught her arm – just as she was about to step into a puddle of grey scummy water. "So do I. So let's try to find out. The hospital said they were letting everyone home today. Why don't we stop in on Tommy and see how he is? He was there; he'll be able to tell us what happened."

"And what about the dreams?" Claire said. "How could we both have similar dreams?"

Patrick shook his head. "I don't know," he sighed. "That's been bothering me most of all."

"I wonder what Tommy Butler dreamed about last night," Claire muttered. She stopped suddenly. Something had moved at the corner of her field of vision.

"What's wrong?"

Claire was about to answer when she caught the flicker of movement again, a hunched shape darting between two unfinished houses. Without turning her head, she looked into Patrick's eyes, seeing herself reflected in his glasses and said, "I think we're being followed."

The boy started to grin, thinking it was a joke ... until he saw that she was serious.

"Don't look around," Claire said as Patrick started to turn his head.

"Why not? It's probably one of the gang from school ..."

His voice trailed away as he realised that most of the pupils had left by the time he came out. "Are you sure you saw something?"

Claire hesitated, then nodded quickly. "I'm sure."

"But that doesn't mean they were following us. Probably just someone else taking a short-cut home."

"Why were they hiding then?" Without giving him time to answer, she said, "What are we going to do?"

"We can turn back ... or go on."

"If we turn back ..." Claire began, but left the sentence unfinished.

Patrick nodded. If there was someone following them – and he wasn't entirely sure that there was – then they would walk right into them. He turned his head to the left and looked down an almost completed side-road. "If we cut through here, we'll get out into the fields. If anyone is following us, they'll have nowhere to hide there. But I think we should just go on as if nothing ..."

A plank of wood fell in one of the houses, the dull slapping noise sounding loud in the afternoon silence. They both turned towards the sound – and saw an ill-defined shape duck down behind a pile of red bricks.

"Do you believe me now?" Claire demanded.

"I never doubted you for a moment," he muttered. Catching hold of her hand, he dragged her down the side-road between rows of houses in various stages of completion. At this end of the road the future houses were little more than outlines traced in cement and blocks on the ground, while further on, piles of brick rose like the skeletal ribs of an ancient dinosaur.

"Don't run," Patrick panted.

"Who's running?" Claire demanded.

"You are."

"Only to keep up with you."

The two teenagers hurried down the unfinished road, squinting in the rapidly fading light, watching the ground for any obstructions or pot-holes.

"If this is someone's idea of a joke, I'll kill them," Patrick muttered grimly as he sank to his ankles in ice-cold mud. It felt disgustingly slimy in his shoes, and squelched with every step.

Claire glanced over her shoulder. "It's not," she breathed in a terrified whisper. She stumbled and fell, dragging Patrick down with her. Hauling her to her feet, he looked back over his shoulder to see what had frightened her ... and felt as if his heart had fallen into the pit of his stomach.

A shape was lumbering down the road after them. A shambling crouched shape that splashed through mud and puddles. It raised its arms as it advanced on the pair ... and they realised that it had no hands.

Patrick and Claire turned and ran.

Chapter Fifteen

Helen Butler glanced up at the clock on the wall as she spun the tap to fill the kettle. Four-thirty. She'd make some tea and take it up to Tommy; he might even be awake by now. He'd been exhausted when the taxi had brought him back from the hospital shortly before noon and she'd made him lie down for a nap. She was expecting him to come down a few minutes later, but when she checked up on him, she discovered that he was sleeping soundly, his breathing deep and rasping, almost a snore.

Helen had got such a fright when the school contacted her yesterday and told her that Tommy and the rest of the class were in hospital. And the more the headmistress had attempted to calm her, the more convinced Helen became that something was seriously wrong. The One O'Clock news on the radio had been rather more reassuring and she'd finally managed to see Tommy late in the evening when she'd driven up to Drogheda with some of the other parents whose children were in the hospital. She wasn't able to hold back the tears when she saw him lying in bed, his skin as pale the sheets. He managed a thin smile and a few whispered words, and then drifted back to sleep again. A young nurse said that they had given him and the rest of the students sedatives to help them sleep and that there was nothing to worry about.

The kettle whistled, startling her.

Helen was staring out into the gathering night, waiting for the small pot of tea to draw, when the doorbell rang. Wiping her hands on a dishcloth she walked out into the hall. Then the phone rang and she picked it up on her way to the door.

"Hello?" Static wailed and crackled down the line before she recognised her husband's voice. "Ed!" Ed Butler worked on an oil rig in the North Sea. "Hang on a second, Ed, someone's at the door." Reaching out, she jerked the door open, then stepped back and picked up the phone again, waving Patrick Elliot and Claire Holland into the hall.

"He's fine," she said into the phone. "He's sleeping now. I was just about to bring him up a cup of tea." She gestured towards the two teenagers, indicating their mud-caked shoes and then pointed to the mat. They rubbed their feet vigorously.

"No. The doctors still don't know what happened. A nurse I spoke to said they just fainted." She put her hand over the mouthpiece. "There's tea made in the kitchen. Bring Tommy up a cup will you?"

Patrick dropped his schoolbag on the floor and disappeared into the kitchen.

Lifting her hand off the mouthpiece, Helen Butler said, "Yes, I'm listening. Patrick and Claire are here. Patrick

Elliot, Claire Holland; they go to school with Tommy. They've come to see how he is." She looked at Claire, who nodded quickly. "Are you sure you'll be home tomorrow?" she continued into the phone.

Patrick re-appeared out of the kitchen carrying two cups of tea. He handed one to Mrs Butler, who smiled gratefully. She watched Claire place her bag on the floor and follow Patrick up the stairs. Tommy's bedroom was at the far end of the landing. She heard them tap gently on the door and Claire whisper, "Maybe he's asleep."

Hinges squeaked as the door opened, then Patrick said softly, "Tommy? Tommy? Are you awake?"

Helen Butler tried to divide her attention between her husband, who was giving her details about his flight the following night, and the sounds coming from upstairs. She heard Patrick's voice rise a notch, sounding surprised and a little puzzled.

"Tommy?"

Helen heard movement on the landing, then someone tapping on the bathroom door.

"Tommy? Are you in there?"

Even before the young couple came pounding down the stairs, their faces pale, eyes wide with fright, she knew something was terribly wrong.

"He's gone," Patrick stuttered. "His bed's empty and he's gone!"

The phone slid from suddenly nerveless fingers and tapped against the wall. Helen shook her head. "He can't be. Tommy?" she called, her voice rising to a shout. "Tommy! Where are you? Tommy!"

But the only response was Ed Butler's tiny voice crackling into the silence that followed.

Chapter Sixteen

They had been touched.

It had entered their souls, their minds, their hearts. It knew their thoughts, their innermost desires, their secret wishes. It shared their dreams and shaped their nightmares.

They were shells now. Empty vessels to do its bidding.

They were nothing ... and yet, and yet ... they were powerful still.

They were the instruments of its release.

Soon.

Chapter Seventeen

By nine o'clock the full extent of the bizarre mystery had unfolded. Tommy Butler was not the only one to have disappeared: the twelve students and their teacher had vanished without trace. The news spread like wildfire through the neighbourhood, bringing people out on to the freezing streets to stand in whispering huddles at their gates, shocked and numbed by the events. All the missing children came from the streets and roads that surrounded the school; everyone knew them or their families and there wasn't a single person in the neighbourhood unaffected by the disappearance.

Police had closed off the streets, and were working through the crowd, taking statements and trying to get people to return to their homes. Dozens of national and international reporters and news crews descended on the small estate, and now swarmed around looking for something to report or film. But with no hard facts, speculation and rumour were running wild.

Patrick and Claire sat huddled together on the stairs in

Tommy Butler's house, listening to the muted cries and sobs coming from the sitting room. The detective in charge of the investigation came out of the room and pulled open the front door. Lights flashed, and the front of the house was lit up as the camera crews turned on their spotlights. Someone began shouting questions, but the police officer folded his arms and ignored them, and gradually the restless crowd fell silent. Lifting a single sheet of paper, he took a deep breath.

"I am Detective Inspector Andrew Whelan; I'm in charge of this investigation. I can now reveal that twelve children and one adult have gone missing. I have to stress that there is no sign of a struggle, no sign that they were forcibly removed or taken against their will." The big man in the rumpled suit glanced down at the sheet of paper again. His bald head gleamed with sweat even though the night was bitterly cold. "I can also confirm," he added very slowly, "that these are the same children and their teacher who were mysteriously struck down in Newgrange yesterday morning."

A buzz of excitement flowed around the group.

"However," the inspector continued, lying confidently, "we are following a definite line of inquiry and we expect results very soon. Now, that's all I have to say at the moment." Without waiting, he turned his back on the barrage of shouted questions, stepped into the hall and closed the door behind him. He was mopping his forehead with a large handkerchief when he spotted the two teenagers sitting together on the stairs. Tucking the handkerchief away, he leaned over the banisters.

"How are you two?"

"Okay," they answered together.

Detective Whelan glanced over his shoulder towards the sitting room where the sounds of heartbroken sobbing could still be heard; someone was asking "Why" over and over again. The parents of the twelve missing children had gathered in the Butler house, drawn together by their common distress. The Christmas tree and festive paper decorations made the tragic disappearances all the more poignant.

"You're Claire Holland and Patrick Elliot." The detective turned the question into a statement. "I'm Detective Inspector Andrew Whelan; I'm heading up this investigation. Call me Andy."

Patrick and Claire looked at him, saying nothing.

The inspector folded his arms across his broad chest and leaned against the wall. "I've been in the force for nearly eighteen years, and I don't think I've ever come across a case like this before." He paused, waiting while a uniformed police officer appeared from the kitchen carrying a tray of teacups. When the door of the sitting room opened, the noise level rose and Patrick and Claire caught a brief glimpse of the distraught parents, including their own, and the school principal, all sitting or standing around the room, faces turned towards the door, hoping for news. When the door closed the inspector turned back to them.

"Do you know who my hero is?" he said suddenly, surprising them. "Sherlock Holmes. I was a great Sherlock Holmes fan when I was about your age. Sometimes I think that's one of the reasons I became a police officer; I wanted to solve crimes like the great detective did. Crimes nowadays aren't like the nice and neat classic mysteries you find in books, they're usually simple, dirty and brutal. But this is different. It's like a big jigsaw," he said sliding the fingers of both hands together. "Fourteen students and their teacher visit Newgrange. Twelve of those students and the teacher are rendered unconscious by some unknown agency. And now those thirteen people have gone missing." His interlaced fingers locked his hands together. "So at the heart of the jigsaw we have Newgrange." He leaned forward. "I want you to tell me what happened yesterday. Everything that happened," he added.

"We've already told the police," Claire said, "a dozen times."

Andy Whelan nodded. "I know. I've read the report. You came out of the mound for fresh air, you smelt something and when you went back inside, everyone was unconscious. Now, tell me what you've left out," he said casually.

"How do you know we've left something out?" Claire asked.

"Because everyone does. You've only told the police what you wanted them to know ... and your stories are just *too* similar," he added with a smile. "Two people in a strange situation will see two different things, come away with different impressions and ideas. But not you two. I think you prepared your story first. Now, what have you not put into the report?"

"Tell him about the tramp," Patrick muttered.

"Tramp! What tramp?" the inspector demanded, looking from Patrick to Claire.

The girl took a deep breath. "There's not a lot to tell. I saw a tramp outside Newgrange yesterday. Patrick had gone for help, leaving me in the mound. I suppose I got scared and went outside. There was a tramp on the other side of the field, watching me. I called to him for help, but he turned away."

"Have you seen him since?" the inspector asked.

"I saw him later hanging around the crowd that had gathered when the police and ambulances had arrived. And then I saw him today," she said softly.

"Today!" The inspector crouched down on his haunches and stared into Claire's wide brown eyes. "Are you sure it was the same tramp?"

"Absolutely. He was standing outside the school watching me, just staring at me. Staring." She shuddered with the memory and Patrick put his arm around her shoulders.

"Someone also chased us through the building site on the way home," Patrick said.

"What! Who?"

Patrick looked at Claire. "We're not sure. It was getting dark."

"Tell me exactly what happened," the inspector said, keeping his voice calm and controlled, not betraying his growing excitement. This might just be the break he was looking for; the two incidents had to be connected.

"I was late getting out of school," Patrick said. "We were taking the short-cut through the building site when Claire spotted someone sneaking along behind us."

"How did you know they were following you?" the inspector asked.

"Because they ducked down whenever we looked back," Claire said.

"Man or woman?"

"Man," they said together.

The inspector nodded. "Please continue."

"We decided we'd make for the fields," Patrick went on, "so that whoever was following us would have no place to hide and would have to show themselves."

"Good idea. Did you get a close look at this person?"

There was a pause. "Just once," Claire said eventually. "I turned around to look, and he was racing after us, arms waving ..."

"And he had no hands," Patrick said in a whisper.

"What do you mean – no hands?" Andy Whelan asked sharply.

"No hands," Patrick said. "His arms were far too long and there were no hands."

"What sort of coat was he wearing?"

"Old, shabby," Claire said immediately.

"A hat?"

Claire nodded again. "A battered hat pulled low over his face."

"And the tramp you saw yesterday – was he wearing a hat also? Could it have been the tramp?"

The teenagers looked at one another, then shrugged. "Maybe," Claire said.

"But what about the hands?" Patrick asked. "We definitely saw no hands."

Andy Whelan grinned. He caught the cuff of his left sleeve and tugged it down, until his hand had disappeared up his sleeve. He waved the empty sleeve at them. "Is this what you saw?"

They nodded.

"I think it was the tramp who chased you. He's probably wearing a coat a few sizes too big, that's why you saw no hands." Straightening his sleeve, he stood up again. "I'm not sure how the tramp is involved – but there has to be some connection. I'll put out his description and we'll haul him in for questioning. If you see him again, steer well clear of him and call the police immediately."

"What's happened to our friends?" Claire asked suddenly. "How could they all just disappear like that?"

Andy Whelan shook his head. "I'm not going to lie to you. I honestly don't know. It looks as if they simply got up and walked out the door. If I were to make a guess, I'd say that they were probably still affected by whatever happened yesterday in the mound. I wish I could find out exactly what went on in there," he added, thinking aloud. "Look, if you remember anything else, no matter how insignificant, I want you to get in touch with me. Oh, and I don't want you going to school tomorrow. You're to stay at home. At the moment you're the only two people who have been to Newgrange and haven't vanished."

"You think someone might have kidnapped the others?" Patrick said quickly.

"And that they might come back for us?" Claire added.

"I didn't say that," Andy Whelan said grimly. "But I'm not going to take any chances."

Chapter Eighteen

"The tape-recorder," Claire said urgently, static crackling on the phone.

"What?" Patrick mumbled, rubbing sleep out of his eyes, coming slowly awake. He had been in the middle of a terrifying nightmare – something about being trapped underground again – when he had heard the phone ringing distantly. Rolling out of bed he had nearly tumbled down the stairs in an effort to get to it before it woke his parents. Slapping on the light with the palm of his hand, he squinted short-sightedly at the clock in the hall, but he couldn't make out the time. "What time is it?"

"Eight-thirty," Claire said brightly.

"Half-eight!" Patrick repeated. It had been after two before he got to bed last night, and at least another hour before he fell into a troubled sleep. He felt wretched. "What time did you get up?"

"Half-seven – as usual," she said. "Patrick. Listen to me, I've thought of something. The tape-recorder. Miss Lee's tape-recorder."

Patrick shook his head, trying to make sense out of what Claire was saying. What tape-recorder? What was she talking about? "Look, can I phone you back? I'm standing here in my pyjamas and I'm freezing. Let me get dressed, make some tea, burn some toast and I'll phone you back." Without giving her a chance to reply, he hung up.

He was climbing back up the stairs when the door of his parents' bedroom opened and his father looked out, blinking sleepily, shading his eyes from the landing lights. "Who was that?"

"Just Claire."

Dave Elliot yawned. "What time is it anyway?"

"Half-eight, Da."

Dave ran his fingers through his thinning hair. "Did you sleep okay last night?"

Patrick shrugged. "Not bad. Why?"

"I could hear you tossing and turning. Bad dreams?" he asked.

Patrick nodded silently.

"They're just dreams, they don't mean anything, just your unconscious mind trying to make sense of the last few days," his father explained.

Patrick nodded again. He knew that, but it didn't make the dreams any less scary. And these dreams were so real. He had been lying under the ground, buried alive ... and he could actually feel the cold earth on his face, granules trickling between his lips, gathering in his nose and ears, clods of earth pressing down on his eyes. "Why don't you go back to bed, Da," Patrick said. "I'm going to get dressed and make some tea. I'll bring you up a cup."

"That would be nice," Dave said, closing the bedroom door. His mother would get up soon, but Patrick knew that he wouldn't see his father again until some time in the afternoon. Since he'd lost his job, he'd been getting up later and later in the day.

Patrick went into his bedroom and pulled the door closed behind him. Picking his clothes up off the floor, he sat on the end of the bed and dressed quickly, shivering in the early-morning chill. The heating hadn't come on and the house was bitterly cold. There wasn't much heating oil left and he knew his parents were trying to make it last as long as possible, especially for the Christmas period when there would be plenty of callers to the house. Pulling on an extra jumper, he went down to the cold kitchen to make tea.

Standing before the grill, watching a single slice of bread slowly toast, he went over his puzzling conversation with Claire. She'd been talking about a tape-recorder. What tape-recorder?

"Miss Lee's tape-recorder," he said aloud. Of course! And then he suddenly laughed, the noise echoing unnaturally in the silent house.

Miss Lee had told the class that she was going to take a tape-recorder with her into Newgrange. She was going to record the "magical experience of the sounds of the sun shining in through the opening," she'd said. Patrick grinned, remembering that he'd asked her how she was going to record the sound of the sun. She'd given him a hundred lines for being so cheeky. Claire had done half the lines for him, effortlessly copying his sloping handwriting.

Munching on a piece of blackened toast, he wandered out

into the hall, picked up the phone and dialled Claire's number.

The phone rang once. "Miss Lee's tape-recorder," Claire said before he even had time to speak.

"You're brilliant," Patrick said, toast crumbs speckling his jumper. "If Miss Lee's tape-recorder was running, recording everything that happened in the mound, it might just give us a clue."

"Exactly," Claire said.

"Shouldn't we tell the police? Inspector Whelan? He seemed okay," Patrick suggested.

"Maybe not just yet," Claire said. "I think we should listen to the tape first, just in case ..." She allowed the sentence to trail away.

Patrick chewed his toast thoughtfully. He knew what the girl was afraid of. The tape might reveal that they had blocked up the entrance. That was probably a crime in itself – defacing an ancient monument. They'd most likely end up being expelled from school – they might even be sent to one of those special schools for difficult children.

"You're right. We've got to get to the tape-recorder first," he said. "Any idea where it is?"

"Probably in Mrs Keogh's office."

"Well, how are we going to get it then? We can hardly walk into her office and ask for it."

"Well, let's think about it."

"You have an idea," Patrick said. "I can tell from your voice."

"I have an idea," Claire agreed, "but I don't want to talk about it over the phone."

Patrick groaned. "That means it could get us into deep trouble."

"We're already in serious trouble," Claire said.

"Don't remind me."

Patrick finished the last of his toast, chewed and swallowed hard, before he asked, "This idea of yours – is it illegal?"

"Absolutely."

"That's what I was afraid of."

Chapter Nineteen

*T*ommy *Butler dreamed.*

He was standing in a barn. His thoughts were confused, disjointed. He remembered waking in his bed, in his own room. The voice, the whispers were all around him, calling him. pulling him out of the bed, and then he was moving – down the stairs and out into the street. There were people all around, but they couldn't see him. The voice was cloaking him, wrapping him in its power. They looked at him, through him. He tried to call to them, but they couldn't hear him. He was being pulled along by the voice, the terrible, terrifying voice. And then later, much later, when he felt as if he had been walking for hours, he had come to the building.

He was bitterly cold because he was wearing nothing more than his light pyjamas and his feet were bare. His toes were so cold he couldn't even feel them, and there was blood and dirt smeared across his toe-nails.

The dream was so real.

So real ...

He could smell the stench of damp and rot from the barn, the sweet odours of mouldering straw and ancient dung, the stink of decaying fruit.

He could hear the squeak of rats all around, the scratching slither of their claws and tails as they scurried across the rafters and burrowed through the straw. And there were other sounds too that might be whispers ... and the whispers wouldn't let him leave.

He knew he wasn't alone in the barn. There were other shapes standing around him, vague, ill-defined shapes. Sometimes they came close enough and he almost recognised them; and there was a taller figure which could be an adult. They, too, seemed to be wearing pyjamas and nightdresses.

Tommy Butler squeezed his eyes shut. He wanted to wake up from this terrible nightmare, but he couldn't.

And the dream was so real that he could taste the salt from the tears that rolled down his cheeks.

Martin Simms dreamed.

He was standing in a barn. He couldn't see too clearly because he wasn't wearing his glasses, but he could hear movement all around him, the rustle of cloth, the sounds of breathing ... and the whispers. And if he listened hard enough, he could almost make out what they were saying.

Jenny French dreamed.

She was standing in a barn. She was cold and wet and very miserable. The dream was so real that she could actually feel the weight of the plaster cast on her arm, the itchy stickiness of the spider's web stuck to her face. She was terrified that at any moment the spider was going to appear.

Jimmy Molloy dreamed.

He was standing in a barn. And he was cold, so cold, so very, very cold. His teeth were chattering so hard that he was afraid they would break.

Helen Lawlor dreamed.

She was standing in a barn. There was a pain in her arm, a dull throbbing ache that numbed her entire arm from fingertip to elbow and when she raised her hand, she could see a thick bandage around her wrist. And yet she couldn't remember what had happened to her wrist ...

Chapter Twenty

"This is not a good idea," Patrick said miserably. "I don't think we should do it."

Claire ignored him. Sitting on the last stair, she pulled on her high-top Nike sneakers and deftly did up the laces. "Well, I'm going, whether you come or not," she said coldly, without looking at him. She had spent the entire day trying to convince him – unsuccessfully. Now that darkness had set in, it was time.

Patrick still favoured talking to Inspector Whelan. "This is serious, Claire. Really serious."

Claire glanced up at him, lips drawn into a thin line. She was sick and tired of his whining. He could be such a wimp at times. "Twelve of our friends are missing. Miss Lee is missing. It doesn't get much more serious than that, Patrick. And it might – just might – be because of something we did. Now, I'm going, with or without you!"

Patrick sighed loudly. Digging his hands into his worn leather jacket, he looked down at his dirty sneakers. "You know I won't let you go on your own," he said eventually.

"It's dangerous, you could get hurt."

Claire looked up mischievously. "Patrick Elliot – are you saying you care about me?"

"I didn't say that," Patrick said quickly. "But if you get hurt – I'll get blamed. I'll come, then, if you insist on doing this. Anyway, someone has to look after you," he added with a smile.

Claire stood up and lifted her heavy red jacket off the bottom of the banister. "And I thought I was the one who looked after you," she grinned. "Right, are you ready?"

"I'm ready."

Claire looked at her watch. "It's eight o'clock now. We have to be back here by nine-thirty at the latest. Mum and Dad should be back from the meeting by ten, and if I'm not here when they get back all hell will break loose."

Patrick nodded. His parents had gone to the same meeting, which had been called by the school to discuss the disappearance of the students. The two teenagers had decided to take advantage of the fact that the school would be open to try and take the tape from Miss Lee's recorder.

"We'd better go out the back way," Claire said, "just in case someone is watching the house." She smiled at Patrick's expression. "Don't look so worried."

"I am worried. I've got a really bad feeling about this," he muttered.

Patrick and Claire slowed when they neared the school. They could see lights blazing in the staff-room and the hall, and the car park was filled to capacity. A long news-van was parked outside the school gates, the satellite dish on the roof pointing to the clear skies.

"We've a problem," Patrick muttered, touching Claire's arm, nodding towards the main entrance. She stared into the shadows for a few moments before she realised that there was a uniformed police officer standing to one side of the double doors. As she watched, his breath smoked on the icy air.

The girl chewed on the inside of her cheek. She had been counting on slipping into the school by the main door while the parents' meeting was underway. The headmistress's office was just beside the door. Then it would be a simple matter of sneaking into the office and extracting the tape from the machine – if it was there! If everything went according to plan, she reckoned they would spend no more then five minutes in the school. But the main entrance was out of the question now.

"What do we do now?" Patrick asked.

"I'm thinking," Claire muttered.

"I've an idea."

"What?"

"We could go home. Give it up," he suggested hopefully.

"The science lab," the girl said suddenly. "Has the broken window been fixed yet?"

"No. I don't think so." One of the small side-windows had been broken three days previously when a cork had blown out of a jar in an experiment. The caretaker had boarded up the window with thin plywood, but they knew from previous experience that it would take a week for the window to be replaced.

"We'll get in that way," Claire said decisively.

"Hang on a sec. The lab is at the other end of the building. We'll have to walk the full length of the school just to get to Mrs Keogh's office ... and then go back the same way. It'll take fifteen minutes at least. We're bound to be caught."

"Don't exaggerate. We won't be more than ten minutes inside." Claire darted across the road to the high metal railing that enclosed the school grounds. Patrick reluctantly ran after her. Following the railing to the left, she turned down a narrow tree-lined street and came to the spot where the metal bars were bowed and spread apart. No-one knew how the bars had become bent, although all new students were told the story that Mr O'Brien, the hulking bear-like maths teacher, had pulled them apart with his bare hands when a student had pushed his head through and got stuck.

Unbuttoning her jacket, Claire shrugged it off and crouched down, squeezing sideways through the narrow opening. When she was on the other side, Patrick passed in her jacket and then unzipped his own. Sucking in his breath, he turned his body sideways and stepped through with his left leg. It was going to be a tight squeeze. He turned his head, feeling the cold rusty metal rasp across his cheek and the bars press against his chest and spine.

A door closed in one of the houses across the narrow street and he heard a car door slam, then the engine start up. Lights came on, illuminating the front of a house, then reversing lights snapped white as the car began to back out of the driveway.

"Come on. Come on!" Claire said urgently. "You'll be seen."

Patrick twisted frantically, trying to move – but he

couldn't. "I'm stuck," he whispered in panic. "I'm stuck!"

The car turned, dipped headlights flooding the narrow street with soft yellow light ... which stopped, less than six inches from the opening in the rails.

"I don't believe it," Claire hissed. Crouching down beside Patrick, she caught his arm, grabbed a handful of jumper – and wrenched him through with all her strength. The bar scraped across his face, skinning his forehead, and dug deeply into his ribs, bruising his spine. "Down!" she said, pushing him to the ground as the headlights washed over the opening.

Patrick lay on the ground desperately trying to stop himself from crying aloud in pain.

"Come on, let's go. We don't have much time." Claire vanished into the shadows.

Climbing stiffly to his feet, Patrick followed her, both hands wrapped around his aching chest. He was sure he'd cracked a rib.

They crept around the side of the school. This area was in total darkness. Reaching into her pocket, Claire pulled out the small torch she had brought and snapped it on, being careful to keep the beam low. The tiny puddle of light danced across the ground. "It looks really different at night," she murmured.

Patrick smiled; he thought he detected a tremor in her voice. "We can always go back."

"Too late for that."

Built in the late 1970s, the school was a modern single-storey prefabricated building, shaped like a square C, with the two laboratories at one end, the offices at the other end and the classes running on both sides of the central corridor. The hall, an ugly rectangular stone block, had been added in recent years beyond the offices.

Claire allowed the torchlight to flicker over the windows. "Where is it?" she muttered.

"Down here," Patrick said.

The girl played the light across the chest-high windows and breathed a quick sigh of relief when she spotted the rectangle of wood. The broken pane hadn't been replaced.

"I'll hold the light," she said, pulling a screwdriver out of her pocket and passing it to the boy.

Patrick slid the tip of the screwdriver in between the edge of the plywood and the windowframe and levered back. The board moved as a small nail shifted. Sliding the screwdriver down a few inches, he levered again, and this time a nail rattled to the floor inside.

"Hurry," Claire insisted.

Patrick ignored her. Working slowly and methodically, he went around the board, gently levering out the nails. When he was satisfied that all the nails were loosened, he passed the screwdriver back to Claire, placed both hands flat against the wood – and pushed. It fell away and rattled to the floor, the noise sounding thunderous in the silence.

The two teenagers froze, hearts thumping, waiting for shouts and lights. Nothing happened.

Without a word, Patrick crouched down and locked his fingers together. Claire slid her foot into his cupped palms and Patrick heaved her up and into the opening. "Watch out for glass," he whispered. When she was inside, he took four steps back, then a short run and launched himself upwards, catching hold of the windowframe and hauling himself up. Claire reached out and pulled him in.

Sitting on the floor, amongst the nails Patrick had prised out, they waited until their hearts had stopped thumping and their eyes had adjusted to the dim light.

"I've just realised that what we've done is called breaking and entering," Claire said grimly. "If we're caught, we are in serious trouble."

Patrick resisted the temptation to say: I told you so.

Chapter Twenty-one

Gnarled and filthy hands gripped the metal rails, cold grey eyes probing the shadows, wondering where the two teenagers had gone.

He had been following them since they had left the girl's house, but had been forced to stay well back because they kept checking behind them, and he'd lost them when they darted across a road.

Why had they returned to the school?

What were they looking for?

Eyes long-used to seeing at night examined the bowed railings, spotting strands of hair clinging to the metal and flakes of rust scattered on the ground. Someone had gone through here – and recently.

Rotting teeth bared in a grin. If they'd gone in this way, then they would have to come out this way. The smile disappeared as the figure faded into the deepest shadows.

Waiting.

Chapter Twenty-two

"It could be locked," Patrick said, gently pressing down on the handle, half-hoping it was. The door clicked open.

Crouching close to the floor, they peered through the half-opened door down the length of the empty corridor. The floor had recently been waxed and it shimmered like glass. The only lights in the darkened corridor were the dull red Emergency Exit signs that gleamed above the side doors, shedding pools of liquid red on the gleaming floors. An oasis of warm yellow light marked the far end of the corridor. It seemed a long way away.

"Keep to the walls," Claire whispered. She pulled the door open, tiptoed out into the corridor and pressed herself up against the wall on her right. In the shadows, she was almost invisible. Easing the laboratory door closed behind him, Patrick stepped out into the corridor and took up position opposite her, his left shoulder against the other wall. He caught the briefest flash of a smile. "Ready?" she whispered.

"Ready."

They set off down the corridor, their rubber-soled sneakers making tiny squeaking sounds on the polished floor. They both found the familiar school strange and different – the deserted classrooms, the unusual shadows and unnatural silence making the place seem alien, almost unreal.

They slowed down as they neared the lighted end of the corridor. They could hear the muted, distant sounds of raised voices in the hall, where the meeting was taking place.

Patrick glanced over at Claire. Although they were still fifteen feet from the end of the corridor, he could see her clearly in the reflected light. She pointed directly ahead towards Mrs Keogh's office.

Patrick mouthed the word 'police' and raised his eyebrows in a question. How were they going to get into the office without alerting the policeman standing outside the open door across from the headmistress's office?

Claire frowned.

And then a door creaked and a figure stepped into the light directly ahead. It was the young police officer. Looking neither right nor left, he rubbed his gloved hands together briskly and disappeared out of sight. Another door squeaked. They both identified the sound: it was the door to the toilets.

"Now!" Claire hissed. Without waiting for Patrick, she darted down the last few feet of the corridor and into the light. Glancing left and right, she tapped gently on Mrs Keogh's door, her ear pressed against the wood, listening for any sounds inside. If she heard any movement, she would turn and run. Pressing down on the handle, she pushed the door open and stepped into the office, then turned and gestured to Patrick, who had remained rooted to the spot.

He was racing down the corridor when the toilet door squeaked open.

With a desperate effort he threw himself forward. He slid into the office just as the policeman stepped out into the corridor. Claire closed over the door, holding tight to the handle, preventing it from clicking shut, and peered out through a crack. She saw the red-cheeked police officer amble back to his post, pulling his gloves on. He stopped directly outside the door and adjusted his cap and turned up his collar before stepping outside into the chilly night to take up his post at the door again.

Claire pressed the door shut quietly, then turned back to the office. The room was in darkness, but they couldn't risk switching on the light. Luckily, the venetian blinds were open, allowing slatted street light into the room. She spotted the tape-recorder immediately. It was on a shelf behind the headmistress's desk. "Easy-peasy," she grinned.

Patrick moved around behind the desk and lifted the small recorder. Tilting it towards the light, he fiddled with it until the top popped up.

"Just grab the tape and let's go," Claire whispered.

"We've got a problem."

Claire looked at him blankly.

Patrick lifted a tiny micro-cassette out of the machine. "My tape-recorder can't handle tapes this small. What about yours?" Claire shook her head. "Do we know anyone who uses one of those tiny pocket recorders?"

The girl shook her head again. "Take the recorder," she

said decisively. She suddenly held up a hand. There were noises in the corridor outside.

Voices.

Drawing closer.

"Mrs Keogh!" she whispered hoarsely. "What are we going to do?"

"Here. Quick." Patrick dropped to the floor.

The girl ran around the desk, sank to the floor and crawled in under the desk beside Patrick. "If she comes in ..." she began.

"She won't ..."

The door opened and the light snapped on, blinding them both. Voices swelled in the corridor outside and they realised that the meeting had finished early. They heard Mrs Keogh wishing someone good-night and then the door closed and footsteps approached the desk.

Patrick wasn't sure which of them was trembling more – Claire or himself – but he could feel his stomach cramp and churn. He was going to be sick.

Paper dropped on to the desk above their heads and they heard the woman sigh loudly. The filing cabinet opened with a squeal and slammed shut, while Mrs Keogh muttered softly to herself. Paper was crumpled noisily, then a wadded ball fell to the ground inches away from Claire. The girl stared at it with wide terrified eyes. If the headmistress came around to pick it up, she would be looking right at them.

The light snapped off and the door closed, leaving the two teenagers in darkness. Patrick leaned his head back against the wood and took a deep breath and Claire started to ease herself out of their cramped hiding place ...

The door opened again. Footsteps thudded across the carpet, and they heard scrabbling on the tabletop above their heads. Then the light went out and the door closed. This time, neither moved until the room was lit up by headlights as a car pulled out of the car park.

Claire crawled out from beneath the desk and crept over to the window to peer through the slatted blinds. "All clear," she called, "even the police have gone."

Patrick came up from beneath the table. His legs felt shaky and muscles twitched in the pit of his stomach. "Close!" he said, wiping greasy sweat from his forehead. His fingers were trembling.

The girl took the tape-recorder from his hands. "We don't have much time. If my Mum or Dad discover I'm missing they'll call out the police and we'll have a lot of explaining to do."

Turning the recorder around, she pressed the *Play* button and slid the volume up.

Nothing happened.

"Did you rewind the tape?" Patrick asked. "Miss Lee must have dropped it, and it probably ran on to the end."

Claire hit *Rewind* and the tape spun. There were several long seconds of silence, before they heard squeaking, squealing high-pitched voices speaking backwards. She hit *Stop* and *Play* and then placed the tape in the centre of Mrs Keogh's desk.

Standing on either side of the desk, Patrick and Claire listened intently.

They heard the sounds of movement and heavy breathing and a dull thud as the tape-recorder bumped against something. Then laughter and voices murmuring softly together. When Miss Lee spoke, her voice was clear and distinct. Claire reached over and lowered the volume slightly.

"I want you to try and imagine what the primitive men who built this place must have thought when they saw the sun slicing through the night to light up the interior of this mound. Remember, they worshipped the sun as a god, they believed in magic, and ..."

There was a short pause.

"Silence! Stop that whispering."

Another pause, and when she spoke again her voice was angry and hard.

"Patrick Elliot. Claire Holland. Stop it at once. Stop that noise immediately."

There was another silence, then she snapped, *"Patrick Elliot ..."*

There was a long silence then a thud and a bang as the tape hit the ground.

"That seems to be it." Claire reached over and rewound the tape.

"Something happened in the mound all right," Patrick said slowly. "Whispering, Miss Lee said. And she obviously thought that you and I were responsible for it. So, whatever was happening wasn't scary ... just different. Unusual."

"She did sound a little frightened," Claire said.

"Just a little," Patrick agreed. "Play the tape again and this time push the volume up to the limit. Let's see if we can we hear anything in the background."

Claire pressed *Play*.

"... and imagine what the primitive men who built this

place must have thought when they saw the sun slicing through the night to light up the interior of this mound. Remember, they worshipped the sun as a god, they believed in magic, and ..."

"Stop!" Patrick snapped. "Did you hear it?"

Claire shook her head. "I heard nothing."

"Rewind. Play it again."

"Remember, they worshipped the sun as a god, they believed in magic, and ..."

"There!"

The girl shook her head again. "I can only hear the tape hissing. What do you hear?"

"Whispering," he said quietly. "It sounds like whispering."

Claire allowed the tape to run on.

"Silence!"

"I hear it," Claire said wonderingly.

"Stop that whispering. Patrick Elliot. Claire Holland. Stop it at once."

The sounds of whispering were clearly audible now, the words nearly distinguishable, the syllables rasping, almost like a beast's growling.

"Who's making those sounds?" Claire wondered. She pulled her coat closed. It was getting cold.

"Stop that noise immediately." Miss Lee's voice was shaking.

The whispering was growing louder. Louder. Louder. It was like a chant, a moaning, grunting chant.

"Patrick Elliot ..."

The whispering was louder now. Clearer.

Patrick looked at Claire. Her eyes mirrored his terror.

Something had been in the mound, something terrible and terrifying, and they had its voice on tape, the voice of something that sounded neither like man nor beast. They each heard different things: a man shouting, a beast snarling, but they both heard the laughter that echoed and echoed around the chamber – and echoed around them now in the headmistress's office.

When the office window cracked and shattered, they both screamed aloud.

Chapter Twenty-three

The window smashed, fragments of glass falling into the room. A second window turned white, then exploded violently, shards of razor-sharp glass flying in the air. Patrick felt a piece bite at his cheekbone, more tangle in his hair. Catching Claire by the hand he dragged her out of the office – just as the rest of the windows paled to a milky whiteness, then erupted inwards, filling the air with deadly pieces of glass.

The tape-recorder continued to run, the mocking voice filling the empty room with terrifying laughter.

"The windows, Patrick, what happened to the windows?"

He shook his head numbly. He dabbed at his stinging cheek, and saw dark blood on his gloves. Then he raised his head, nostrils flaring. "Do you smell something?"

Claire breathed deeply, then coughed as her stomach rebelled at the rancid stink. "The Newgrange smell!"

The bitter odour filled the hall, a stench that was both foul and sweet, like rotting fruit.

"And it's got so cold," Claire said quietly, her breath

billowing whitely before her face. It hadn't been this cold a few moments ago. Maybe the heating had been turned off – but when she touched the radiators, she found that they were still warm. She had been staring at the glass entrance doors before she realised what she was seeing. The glass was turning milky, opalescent, as if a thick fog was billowing up outside. But this wasn't fog. She could actually see the swirls and whorls of ice forming on the glass, thickening into beautiful twisting patterns. "Look," she breathed.

"It's the sudden cold ..." Patrick began, teeth chattering. "The sudden cold shattered the windows." He caught the girl's arm and dragged her forwards and down, covering her body with his. The glass doors shattered, raining shards of glass down on them, ripping his leather jacket, slicing into his jeans. Hauling her to her feet, he pulled her down the corridor, glass crunching underfoot. The intense cold was a physical thing now, stealing the air from their lungs, sending icy fingers deep into their flesh, numbing hands and feet, dulling their thoughts, slowing them down.

Glass creaked, turning milk-white, then cracked as they raced past, windows shattering along both sides of the corridor, the sounds like gunshots. A glass display case caved in, the doors crumbling in their wake into what looked like granules of sand. A skylight broke, spears of toughened plastic raining down into the corridor, foot-long slivers embedding themselves in the wooden floor behind them. A pressurised fire extinguisher shuddered on the wall, then ruptured, spewing white foam across the walls and floor, splashing them both. Patrick felt the foam burning into the cuts on the backs of his legs.

"We've got to get out ..." he said desperately.

"Back to the lab."

The lights flickered on, glowing brightly, blinding them both, then dimmed to little more than sparkling embers before blazing brightly again. The flourescents crackled and buzzed, then detonated into dust in a rattling chain of explosions.

The teenagers ran hunched-over now as the sharp gritty dust filled the air. They were running blind, with sparkling after-images from the lights still dancing on their retinas.

The sprinkler system came briefly to life, water spurting, then freezing ... and then the pipes feeding the system burst open as the water in them froze solid. The heavy pipes slit horizontally like paper and pulled away from the ceiling, dangling in mid-air like spears. Claire brushed by one and felt the ragged end rip at the shoulder of her jacket, peeling away a curling strip of material. She shuddered, knowing what would happened if either of them ran straight on to one of the broken pipes.

Water suddenly bubbled up from beneath the floor as the underground pipes split. It froze immediately, forming a thin coating of glass-impregnated ice on the polished wood, making their footing treacherous and a fall deadly.

Patrick's hand hit the handle on the laboratory door so hard that it hurt. The handle snapped off. Standing back, he kicked the door with the flat of his foot, and the entire lock ripped away. They threw themselves into the laboratory and slammed the door behind them.

But the deadly chill followed.

Beakers and test tubes popped and shattered in a series

of mini explosions and then the enormous windows creaked as they turned white. The two teenagers threw themselves to the floor under the high teacher's desk before the windows blew inwards, sweeping the benches clean of all equipment; fragments of glass rattled around the room, embedding in the walls, coating the blackboard in sparkling dust. A water pipe beneath the sink burst, a sudden geyser of water spurting upwards, freezing immediately.

"Patrick!" Claire whispered urgently.

The boy nodded. He too had smelt the noxious odour of gas. One of the gas taps had ruptured. "We've got to get out – now!"

They darted across the room, stumbling over the laboratory equipment scattered on the floor. In her haste, Claire almost fell, but Patrick caught her and held her steady until she got a grip on the frame and then dropped to the ground. Patrick followed her.

It was even colder outside. The air was so sharp it burned their lungs, hurt their eyeballs, made their fillings ache. Claire's numb fingers fumbled with her small torch, snapping it on. The beam of light danced off a thick hoarfrost which covered the ground. "That wasn't there when we came in," she muttered.

There was a dull thump from the laboratory, followed by a flash, and then they heard the crackle of fire. "The chemicals," Patrick whispered. He grabbed Claire's shoulder and dragged her away from the school building and around by the back of the bicycle sheds. When they looked back they saw that all the windows in the school were broken, jagged glass jutting in every window frame.

Pressing her scarf to her mouth, Claire asked over and over, "What happened, what happened?"

Patrick shook his head. Everything had been fine until ... "The tape," he said slowly. "Everything was fine until we played the tape."

Claire shuddered, remembering the terrifying whispers. "I've heard those whispers before," she said very slowly. "I heard them in the mound. And I heard them again on the phone when I tried to call you the night we came back from Newgrange. And I've heard them in my dreams."

"So did I," Patrick admitted, "the same whispers."

A tremendous explosion shook the whole school. The laboratory was engulfed in a fireball, long tendrils of liquid fire darting out of the broken windows, splashing on to the ground. A section of the roof flew off.

"The gas bottles," Patrick shouted above the roar of the flames. Red-hot cinders rained down on them.

"Patrick, what have we done?" Claire cried as they staggered away from the blazing building.

Patrick didn't answer the question. Taking a deep breath he pushed his way through the opening in the bars, ignoring the tight squeeze, terror lending him speed. Claire followed, climbing roughly through.

And suddenly there was a shape in front of them, a tall, foul-smelling shape that wrapped black-nailed fingers in their coats and dragged them forward into the light. A reeking breath washed over them. "You have no idea what you've done."

Chapter Twenty-four

A tremendous explosion lit up the night sky, bathing the terrifying figure in lurid red light.

"The tramp!" Claire said, her voice disappearing into a breathy whisper.

A creased and lined face the colour of old leather stared down at them. Hard grey eyes, that seemed far too young for the face, regarded them coldly. "I'm not going to harm you – though by rights I should toss you back into the flames for what you've done." The tramp released his grip and pushed them away. "If you want to know what happened in New-grange two days ago ... if you want to know what's happening now, then follow me." He turned away without another word and was quickly swallowed up into the night.

Shaken and terrified, Patrick and Claire looked at one another. Behind them, another explosion detonated, shattering windows in the houses across from the school. Long streamers of flame rained down on the street, a dozen tiny fires taking hold on roofs and in gardens. The night came alive with sirens, with shouts, screams and curses, car-horns blaring, burglar alarms belling, a sliding screeching crash as two cars collided on the main road.

"What have we done?" Claire asked again.

Reaching out, Patrick took her hand in his, and they set off after the tramp.

Sitting in what would eventually be a kitchen in one of the half-finished houses across from the school, Patrick and Claire looked fearfully at the tramp. Light from the blazing school lit up the room, throwing dancing shadows across the walls, giving him an elongated stick-like shadow. They watched in silence as he dragged up blocks of cement to form makeshift seats. He was older than they had first thought, smaller too, and his hands and wrists, where they protruded from the voluminous coats he wore, looked frail and tiny. But he carried the heavy blocks with surprising ease. Firelight danced off his shabby broken-brimmed hat, occasionally highlighting a gleaming eye, or the stub of a rotten tooth. Even from across the room, they could smell the stale odour off him, a mixture of sweat, decay and damp grass.

The tramp sat on one of the piles of blocks and glanced to his right through the empty window. The lower half of the school was engulfed in flames, and four units of the Dublin fire brigade were desperately attempting to keep the blaze under control and prevent it spreading any further.

"I don't think there will be school tomorrow," he said grimly.

The teenagers smiled shakily.

"But then, there may not be a tomorrow," the tramp added, very softly.

"What do you mean?" Claire asked. She sat on a pile of blocks facing the old man. "Who are you?"

"I am known as Nathan Keeper," he said and paused. "You are Claire and you are Patrick. Oh, don't look so alarmed; I heard you call each other by those names."

Patrick crouched down beside Claire. Flames reflected off his glasses, turning them crimson. "Mr Keeper, you have to tell us what happened in the school."

"You may call me Nathan. Keeper is a title, not a proper name. I know what happened, but tell me what you did before ..." he waved a long-nailed hand at the flames, "before all this."

"It started in Newgrange," Claire said. "But you know what happened in Newgrange. You were there."

Nathan Keeper nodded. "I was there. I am always there."

"You know our teacher and friends have gone missing?" Patrick said.

"I know that too." He looked at Claire. "Continue."

"Our teacher, Miss Lee, had a tape-recorder with her. We knew she'd been recording everything that went on in the mound and we thought if we could hear the tape it might give us a clue as to what happened."

"So you played the tape."

Patrick nodded. "We played the tape."

"And what did you hear?"

"Whispers," Claire said very softly, her own voice barely above a whisper, "whispers and laughter."

"And then it got so cold ... and the glass shattered," Patrick said.

Nathan Keeper turned his head to look at the school

again. When he spoke, his voice was quiet, distant, almost as if he was speaking to himself. "You see, such is his power, that even a recording of his voice can draw down the elements ..." Suddenly realising that the two teenagers were watching him, he turned back. "You heard the voice of Crom Cruach," he said simply. "The Great Evil." The tramp's lips peeled back from the stubs of his rotting teeth. "And because of you, he is about to come into this world again," he snarled. He surged to his feet, white spittle flecking his lips. "You've just seen what his voice alone can do – and this is but a tiny fraction of his power. Before the sun shines again, Crom Cruach will rise from his tomb beneath the House of the Dead, and claim this world as his own." Nathan Keeper jabbed a finger at them. "You have sentenced this world to an eternity of agony!"

Chapter Twenty-five

I t was time.

It sent its consciousness into the countryside, seeking the thirteen chosen ones. It found them waiting patiently where it had taken them, in a rotting building close to the countryside. Although their bodies were still and unmoving, their thoughts were wild, their nightmares terrifying. It took their dreams and terrors, feeding off the emotions, savouring them, drawing strength from them.

It was time.

Come.

Come.

Come to me ...

Watching through the eyes of the female

adult, it saw them moving, their limbs jerking raggedly like broken puppets. It urged them onwards, faster and faster, pushing them to a pace no normal human could keep up. But these were no longer human. It had claimed them now ... as servants ... slaves ... food.

Walking through the night at this pace, they would reach the House of the Dead in the dark hours before the dawn. Before the sun rose.

And then ...

And then ...

Freedom.

Chapter Twenty-six

"Let me tell you what you've done," Nathan Keeper continued. He stopped and took a deep breath, visibly calming himself. "When you prevented the sun from shining in through the light-box in the House of the Dead – the place you know as Newgrange – you broke a *geas*, a binding, a spell that was ancient long before the monument rose out of the Irish countryside."

In the empty shell of the building, the old man's voice swelled, filling the room.

"You set in motion a train of events that will ultimately lead to the destruction of the known world. Oh, you smile, boy," he hissed at Patrick, poking him in the chest with a stiff finger. "You smile. You think I'm nothing more than a crazy old man?" He waved a hand at the blazing school. "So tell me how that happened? You played the tape and heard Crom Cruach's voice ... and the sound of that voice alone was enough to draw down the bitter chill and destroy your school. And remember, what you felt tonight was the merest shadow of the god's power." Nathan Keeper spun away and leaned stiff-armed on the window-ledge. He turned his face back towards them, and firelight washed it red and black, wiping away the wrinkles and grime, hinting at the handsome man he had been in his youth.

"Crom Cruach. When he walked this world, Crom Cruach was known as the Great Evil ... and evil is cold, cold, cold. Evil sucks the light and heat from a body, leaving it an empty shivering shell. Since the dawn of time, warriors have spoken of the chill of the battlefield. Alexander felt it when he conquered the world, the Great Khan rode with it from the steppes of Mongolia, the Crusaders carried it with them into the Holy Land. In this century, when countless men died in the fields of Flanders and on the beaches of Normandy, the newspapers always reported that it was cold.

"Crom Cruach will take the heat from this world, turning it into a frigid shell, colder than the dark side of the moon. But do you know what is all the more terrible? The Great Evil will ensure that the human-kind remains alive. It will allow them to live shadows of their former lives, to continue their petty wars, to create and destroy, to grow and multiply, to fill the world. It will feed off their emotions, off their fear and terror, their hate, and when it grows hungry for something more substantial, it will feed off their flesh."

The old man's smile was terrifying.

"You doubt me. I can see it in your eyes. Are you going to ignore the evidence of your own senses? Will you try to claim that the smoking ruin across the road burned down accidentally? And your friends, how do you account for their disappearance? Will you also attempt to rationalise away your dreams, your nightmares about being trapped underground, the whispers you heard? You heard them because you came close to the wakening god, your dreams are but a hint of his reality."

Nathan Keeper turned back to look through the empty window at the burning building. When he continued, his voice was softer, the trace of a rural accent obvious.

"You live in the last years of the twentieth century. In your homes you have access to technology that would have seemed magical to your own grandfathers. In this technological age where everything has an explanation, it is fashionable not to believe in gods. It is easy to forget that civilisations rose and fell worshipping gods and fearing demons, that some of the greatest inventions of this age were made possible by inventors who believed in a god or gods. Were all those people wrong, are all the myths and legends nothing more than fairy stories?" He spun around, his eyes glittering. "Gods once walked this world. Non-human, powerful, beautiful ... deadly. But you don't want to know about gods and demons, do you? No, I suppose you don't," he said softly. "But let me tell you this: the gods never die.

"When ice covered most of this planet, the human-kind who lived in caves and huddled in valleys in this part of the world worshipped Crom Cruach. Some worshipped him as a god, others claimed he was a demon. The first sheaf of wheat, the first fruits – and sometimes even the first-born, both human and animal – were offered to him."

Nathan Keeper threw his head back and his voice rose again, powerful and majestic.

"When the climate changed and the warm winds from the south blew across this land, the god's power weakened. This land was invaded by newcomers, dark-skinned strangers from the warm lands around the Middle Sea, red and blond-haired warriors from the northern climes. They brought with them their own gods and goddesses; they had no time for a god who exhulted in evil, who fed off fear and terror, who demanded such terrible sacrifices.

"There were many battles and at times priests of the Great Evil seemed to be triumphant and chill winter would claim the land, but always the warrior-magicians of the new gods fought back, bringing summer to the fields again.

"For many years the battle swayed back and forth. Some of it was fought on the fields of men, but more often it was carried on in dreams and nightmares, and only the elements would bear testament to the identity of the victors – sunshine or winter chill.

"Although Crom Cruach's strength was stronger in winter, it was on a night like this, with a clear sky and the stars sharp and sparkling, that we defeated the Great Evil. Like many gods he was arrogant, and never expected that we would dare attack him in his den in the middle of winter. But he was wrong.

"I led a troop of warrior-priests into the heart of his lair. None of us expected to come out. The battle was brief, but bloody, and at times I thought that the few human-kind would surely fall against the might of the god and his minions, many of whom were neither man nor beast.

"But we knew that if we failed, then the Great Evil would claim the world, and our fear lent us strength and courage. Courage enough to finish him.

"We couldn't kill Crom Cruach for he was a god and we,

despite our great powers, still only humans.

"When we put the creature into the ground, we bound it there with carved stone and cold soil. Later, we raised the earth atop the cairn, and wove into the fabric of the place an ancient spell to keep the beast at bay, the pure light of the sun renewing the spell each year, driving him deeper underground.

"We knew he was not dead, for that which does not live cannot die.

"We knew he was waiting, festering in the earth, waiting for the spell to be broken."

Nathan Keeper spun around to look at them. "And when you covered the light-box; when you prevented the sun from shining into the heart of the mound and rekindling the ancient magic, you broke the spell." The old man seemed about to say more, then he simply turned back to look at the fire.

The two teenagers were silent for a few moments, trying to absorb the tramp's wild ramblings. Finally, Patrick said, "You keep saying 'we' as if you were there ..."

"I was," the old man said softly. "I told you – I led the final assault on Crom Cruach. I was one of those who put the god into the ground."

Claire laughed shakily. "But that would make you ..."

"Ancient? Yes, I am ancient. I am old, old beyond time, old beyond imagining. I was ancient when the pyramids rose out of the deserts, when Rome was nothing more than a scattering of huts on the banks of a muddy river. I have seen civilisations rise and fall ... and now I suppose I am destined to see this one crumble too. And my only regret is that I have failed."

"How?" Claire asked.

"I am Nathan the Keeper. It was my task to ensure that the spell was renewed every year."

Patrick shook his head. "And what about those years when the sun didn't shine through the opening? What about cloudy years?" he demanded, his voice rising triumphantly.

"The sun is always there, clouds or not. In my time I would have said that the magic of the light passed through the clouds into the heart of the mound. But in these modern times, I suppose I should say that the ultra-violet rays passed into the mound. But no-one has ever deliberately blocked the opening before."

"I've never heard such rubbish in all my life," Patrick said flatly.

"I don't care what you believe," Nathan Keeper said mildly. "I am old now, old and tired. Maybe I'm glad it's coming to an end. In a few hours nothing will matter at all."

Chapter Twenty-seven

"I believe you."

Patrick turned to look at Claire, eyes wide in astonishment. "You what?"

"I believe him," she said simply.

Patrick's mouth opened and closed as he attempted to think of something to say.

The girl stood up and turned back to Nathan Keeper. "What happens now?"

The old man shrugged. "Crom is controlling the twelve children and the adult. I would imagine that they are already on their way to the House of the Dead to dig him out of the heart of the mound."

"Why can't he come up himself?"

"The mound has existed for five thousand years. But we put the god into the ground long before that. He has lain in the earth for so long now that he is weak." The old man sighed. "But when you covered the opening for those few minutes, it gave the god enough time to touch your friends with his mind, to slide deeply into their thoughts and dreams. It was the shock of his invasion into their minds that stunned them. The stink you smelled was the odour of ancient rotting power. Once Crom was controlling their dreams, he was controlling them. Your friends are alive and aware, but they think that everything that is happening to them is a dream, a terrible, terrifying nightmare from which there is no escape. They are on their way to Newgrange. When they reach the mound, they will dig him out with whatever tools they have, and with their bare hands if necessary ..." He stopped suddenly.

"And then?" Claire asked.

Nathan Keeper shook his head.

Claire caught his sleeve, forcing him to turn and look at her. "What then?" she demanded.

"The god will be weak ... he will need sustenance," the old man whispered. "Food."

Claire pressed both hands to her mouth, suddenly realising what he was saying. "You mean ... *them!* We've got to stop him."

Nathan Keeper laughed drily. "You might as well try to stop the wind."

"But you stopped him once before."

He shook his head. "That was long ago ... in a different world."

Claire rounded on Patrick. "We must get to Newgrange."

"What! You're out of your mind."

The girl looked at him, her lips drawn into a thin line, her eyes dark and angry.

"Don't listen to him, Claire, he's mad," Patrick whispered urgently. Catching her arm, he drew the girl away from the tramp who was still staring at the fire. "Claire, can't you see he's talking nonsense. Gods and demons, warrior-priests, magic! His mind has gone. Drink or drugs, I suppose."

"I believe him, Patrick," Claire said slowly.

"Drunken ravings!"

"What about the school?" she snapped. "How do you account for what happened in there?" She touched a long tear in his leather jacket.

"It was an accident, a freak accident."

"And our friends! Where have they gone, what's happened to them? How can thirteen people just disappear like that?" she demanded.

Patrick opened his mouth to reply, but Claire pressed on.

"And the dreams, what about the dreams ... and the whispers?"

"I'm sure there is a rational explanation for all this ..." he began.

"Patrick, I want you to drive us to Newgrange."

He shook his head firmly. "Listen to yourself. Listen to what you're saying."

"We can take Mum's car. You can drive."

Patrick continued shaking his head.

"We should be there in an hour or so," she insisted.

"No way," Patrick said firmly. "This has gone far enough. I allowed you to bully me into coming to the school with you, but I'm not getting involved in anything else. And especially not because of the demented ramblings of a drunken tramp! Well, I won't do it, not even for you. And you're a fool if you go!"

"So, I'll be a fool then! But at least I'll have tried."

"Suit yourself. You usually do." Patrick pulled away from her and stepped out into the darkened hallway.

Claire listened to his footsteps echoing on the bare floor-boards, expecting him to come back at any moment. They'd had arguments like this before, but always made up. When she eventually realised that he wasn't going to return this time, she turned back into the room. Nathan Keeper was looking at her, arms folded across his chest, eyes unreadable beneath the shadow of his hat. "Is there anything we can do at Newgrange?" Claire asked.

The old man shook his head. "I don't know," he admitted.

"But at least we have to try."

Nathan nodded. "We have to try. That's all we can do."

Patrick wandered down the side-streets, feeling his anger and frustration churn and bubble inside him. Why couldn't she see that the tramp was nothing more than a drunken old fool? His dreams of gods and demons came out of a bottle of cheap cider. He was probably dangerous too.

And he'd stormed off and left Claire with him.

She'd be all right. She was always all right. Even when they landed in hot water, she usually managed to come out of it without too much trouble, whereas he always got the worst of it. She could charm herself out of anything. But this was different. This was serious. And they always stood by each other. But now he had left Claire alone with the mad old fool.

Patrick slowed down. So she wanted to take her mother's car and drive up to Newgrange ... and then what? What was

131

she going to do when she realised that she was alone in the middle of a field with the madman?

Patrick stopped, leaning against the cold metal of a lamp-post.

How would he be able to live with himself if anything happened to her? She was such a part of his life, and had been for as long as he could remember. He didn't want to think of anything happening to her; he didn't even want to begin to think of a future without her. He realised now that his earlier anger had been fear; he had been frightened, frightened for her, frightened for both of them.

By the time he got back to the building site, the house was empty. Claire and the tramp had disappeared.

Claire stopped at the top of the road and peered around the corner. Her father's van was in the drive, while her mother's Toyota was parked on the road outside. There was a police car parked beside it. The house was ablaze with lights, and there seemed to be a lot of people inside, milling about in confusion. So, they knew she was missing. Well, it was too late to go back now. Darting across the narrow road, she turned down a side-lane. Nathan Keeper followed her.

Claire stopped in the laneway at the back of her house and stood on her toes to peer over the top of the gate. She could see into the dining room. Her mother was standing by the fireplace; her head was bent and her shoulders were shuddering and Claire realised that she was weeping. The girl felt guilty. She hated seeing her mother like this; she wanted to run into the house and wrap her arms around her, tell her that everything was all right. But she couldn't.

"Stay here," she whispered.

"What are you going to do?" Nathan asked.

"The spare keys to Mum's car are in the cupboard beside the fridge. I'm going to sneak in and grab them, then we can head off to Newgrange."

"Can you drive?" Keeper asked.

Claire shook her head.

"Neither can I."

The girl took a deep breath. "I've watched my mother do it often enough and she's shown me what to do. I'm sure I'll managed it," she said with more confidence than she felt. Easing up the catch on the gate, she slipped into the darkened garden. She knew she was safe enough; even if her mother turned and looked through the window, she wouldn't see further than a few feet.

The girl made it to the garden shed, then stopped. There was no-one in the kitchen. It would take her about twenty seconds to get inside and grab the keys. She wasn't sure what she was going to do if someone saw her. Turn and run probably.

She darted forward. When she and Patrick had left earlier – and it seemed so long ago now – they'd left the back door unlocked. She hoped it was still open. It was.

The kitchen smelt warm and comfortable. She could hear the buzz of voices from the dining room, the sound of her mother weeping, her father speaking in short angry sentences. A phone shrilled in the hall, and was picked up immediately. The cupboard door squealed as she opened it. The keys jangled when she lifted them. Clutching them in her hand, she tiptoed back to the door and was just pulling it closed behind her when the kitchen door opened and her mother stepped into the room. For a single instant mother and daughter stared at one another, eyes wide with shock.

"Claire!" Moira Holland breathed thankfully.

The girl turned and ran.

"Claire!" Her mother's cry was a mixture of despair and puzzlement as she saw her daughter disappear into the night.

Claire and Nathan raced down the narrow lane, shouts and cries following in their wake. They slowed to a walk when they reached the street; but when they saw it was empty they started running again. They had actually reached the old Toyota before they realised that there was someone sitting on the ground beside it.

"Someone has to look after you," Patrick Holland said, coming to his feet.

Chapter Twenty-eight

T ommy Butler knew where he was going now: to Newgrange, the House of the Dead.

He was tired, so tired. How could he be dreaming and
feel tired?

His entire body was in agony. How could he feel pain in
a dream? How could it hurt when he fell to the ground,
skinning hands and knees, how could his feet hurt so much
with every step he took? He had looked back once when he'd
fallen, and seen bloody footprints on the ground. It was a
long time later before he realised that he had left those
marks. It was easier walking on grass, the cool dampness
soothed his raw feet, and they had been walking on grass
for a long time now, cutting across fields, pushing their way
through hedgerows, splashing through bitterly cold streams.

Someone stumbled into him — a girl, and she looked
vaguely familiar... He was still struggling to remember her
name when she slipped again and he immediately forgot
about her.

Tommy stopped. He was aware of people standing still

around him. They were waiting ...

As one, they turned, faces raised to the night sky ... and looked across the sparkling fields to the ancient House of the Dead.

Their sigh was like the sound of a single voice, a mixture of relief, of joy, of triumph.

It was over.

Chapter Twenty-nine

They drove in silence through the empty suburban streets. Patrick and Claire sat in the front of the small car, while Nathan Keeper sat in the back, peering between the front seats. In the close confines of the car, the smell from the old man was appalling and Patrick rolled down the window to allow the chill night air to blast in, even though it numbed the right side of his face.

"You are smelling decay," Nathan Keeper said with a bubbling laugh. The laughter turned into a liquid cough. "I have lived too many years beyond my time. My powers have faded and my body can no longer renew itself, so it is breaking down. Thus I am destined to live forever in this decaying shell. You will not believe me I know, but I was once proud of my looks ... it has been many years now since I last looked in a mirror."

"Why did you remain behind?" Claire asked. She winced as Patrick crunched the gears, the engine howling.

"Nothing lasts forever. The spell we put on the god had to be regularly renewed," Nathan said simply. "It was easier

137

in the past when the human-kind still worshipped gods. I became a priest of whatever religion they worshipped and always ensured that the ceremony at the House of the Dead was incorporated into their beliefs. In those early years, the binding spell was powerful indeed, powerful enough to drive Crom Cruach deeper and deeper into the ground. Once, I had great hopes that I would be able to give up my task or pass it on to another priest ... but the world was changing around me and I didn't realise it." He laughed again. "When Christianity began to take hold in Ireland, marking the beginning of the end of the old ways, when men no longer worshipped at Newgrange, when only a few would gather to pay homage to the sun, I knew then that like Crom Cruach, I too was doomed to an eternity of suffering." He touched Patrick on the shoulder. "Turn here. This is the road to the House of the Dead."

Chapter Thirty

It was close to two-thirty in the morning when they reached Newgrange. Patrick pulled the car into the side of the road and turned off the engine, breathing an enormous sigh of relief. Driving the strange car at night on icy roads had been a nerve-wracking experience and he was bathed in cold sweat.

Across the fields, Newgrange rose out of the dark landscape like a slumbering beast, the quartz set into its white walls, sparkling like stars.

"Was this how it looked in your day?" Claire asked Nathan Keeper.

The old man shook his head. "No. This is ... too pretty," he said eventually.

"What do we do now?" Patrick asked quietly. He looked around. "I don't see signs of anyone," he couldn't resist adding.

"That's because you're not looking," Nathan said. Leaning across Patrick's shoulder he pointed through the windscreen. "What do you see?"

"Nothing. A field."

"What else?"

Patrick shook his head. "Nothing."

Claire drew in her breath sharply. She had suddenly seen what Nathan was talking about. "Patrick, look at the grass ... it's sparkling silver with frost ..."

"Oh," Patrick breathed. He felt as if he'd been kicked in the stomach. The grass in the fields surrounding Newgrange was a shining silver carpet ... except for dozens of black footprints that led straight into the mouth of the mound.

Claire pulled open the door and stepped out.

"Where are you going?" Patrick almost tumbled out of his own door in his haste to join her.

"Our friends are inside. We've got to get them out. We've got to stop them digging up Crom Cruach." She turned to Nathan who was slowly and stiffly climbing out of the car. "You defeated the Great Evil before. How did you do it?" she demanded.

"With courage. That is the only way humans can overcome evil." The old man set off across the fields, Patrick and Claire following him. "Crom will be weak now, very weak. Controlling thirteen of the human-kind will have drained the last of his energy. He will be particularly vulnerable in the first few minutes when he rises from the ground. But once he has fed, he will be invincible."

They slowed as they neared the entrance to the mound. Claire flicked on her torch, playing it across the huge gate stone with its intricate carved spirals. There was a bloody hand-print on the stone, the blood shining red and black in the torchlight. Claire silently measured the span of the hand

140

with her own – it was exactly the same size.

"If you could bring your friends out," Nathan said slowly, "then perhaps I could use some of the old magic of this place to break Crom's spell."

The girl moved her torch across the entrance. Blood sparkled on the walls and floor. Then the light flickered and died.

"The god is close," Nathan whispered. He shivered suddenly. "He is coming. I can feel it. Stay here," he said and hurried across the field, making for a line of bushes.

Claire turned to Patrick. "I'm scared," she said.

"Me too," he said. His teeth were chattering, but he tried to convince himself that it was only the cold.

"Thanks for coming," she said eventually.

"You know I wouldn't let you do this on your own. I was scared something was going to happen to you." Patrick was about to say more when Nathan re-appeared. He was holding two long branches. The ends of both had been wrapped around with thick cloth which stank of petrol.

"Your torch is unreliable near Crom Cruach," Nathan said, handing them each a stick. He pulled out a box of matches and struck a light. When he held it to the padded ends of the torch, they popped alight, the flames sparking wildly, warm yellow light flooding the entrance.

Patrick shoved the blazing torch into the entrance. Shapes and shadows danced up the walls.

"Are you coming?" Claire asked the old man.

"I cannot," he said simply. "The mound is a magical place. If I was to step inside, it would wipe away the ancient spell that has kept me alive this long. I have to remain here."

Claire nodded. "We'll bring our friends out."

"You don't have much time," Nathan said. "Listen – what do you hear?"

"Nothing," she said finally.

"That's because there is nothing to hear. The birds and beasts know the Great Evil is coming."

They could feel an increase in temperature as they advanced slowly down the narrow passage. The air was warmer, heated also by the torches their carried, the tips of the flames licking the low ceiling, the smoke stinging their eyes.

Patrick, who was in the lead, stopped twice to look at bloody hand-prints smeared on the walls, and there was plenty of evidence that many bloody feet had moved along the passageway. He was shaking now, his whole body trembling with absolute terror, a sour sick feeling in his stomach, a pounding at the base of his skull. When he glanced over his shoulder at Claire, he knew by the tight expression on her face that she was feeling the same.

He stopped when he heard the sound.

"I hear it," Claire said, before he could ask the question.

The rasping, twisting, hissing sounds echoed softly down the passage. There was also a sound of grinding, as if heavy stones were being dragged one across the other.

And there were whispers.

Urgent, triumphant whispers.

They knew what they were hearing long before they came out into the central chamber: their friends were digging up Crom Cruach.

"Hurry," Claire pushed Patrick forward, the flame from

142

her torch singeing his hair.

He moved quickly through the twisting passage, turned, disappeared from her sight, and then she heard him cry out – a wordless exclamation of horror. She rounded the corner and stood at the entrance to the central chamber.

Raising her torch high, she looked upon a scene from a nightmare.

Her friends, boys and girls she had grown up with, had gone to school with, played with – her teacher too – were unrecognisable. Wearing rags of clothes, filthy, their bare feet caked with mud and blood, they knelt on the hard floor in the centre of the chamber and scrabbled in the dirt with their bare hands. Their eyes were wide and unblinking, and they had been working in total darkness, clawing at the earth with raw hands, and broken fingernails. They had scooped out a deep depression in the centre of the floor, and were now starting to pull up thick stone slabs.

And the whispering was all around them, the words sliding together, hissing, rasping.

> "Hurry. Hurry.
> "Hurryhurryhurryhurry ...
> "I am coming, coming,
> "comingcomingcoming ..."

Little Jenny French staggered blindly past them, balancing a chunk of stone on the filthy plaster-cast on her arm. She dropped the stone on a pile in the corner and moved sluggishly back for more.

Patrick grabbed her, pushing her towards Claire. "Get her out of here," he snapped, his terror solidifying into cold anger. These were his friends, and yet they were moving and acting like mindless beasts.

And it was his fault.

Claire caught Jenny by the arm and pulled her back into the passage. She went unresistingly, but her head turned and she looked with blind eyes at the others.

There were tears streaming down Claire's face as she pulled Jenny out into the bitter night air. It was hard to tell just how serious the girl's injuries were. Her feet and legs were terribly marked and her hands were all bloody and skinned where she had torn at the earth.

Nathan took the girl from Claire's hands. His lined face creased in pain when he saw her injuries. Leading her into a circle he had traced out on the brittle grass, he pressed his fingers to her face and the lines of strain and fear faded as her eyes closed. "Go, get the others," he said tiredly.

When Claire reached the inner chamber again, she found her friends blundering around in confusion. Patrick had pulled most of them off the floor on to their feet, but as soon as he got one up, another would drop down again.

The whispering had reached a crescendo, the single word – *hurry* – bouncing round and round the room until it was barely distinguishable.

Claire caught the nearest boy – Jimmy Molloy – and pulled him out into the passage. She wished she could take more at a time, but she needed one hand to hold the torch. Jimmy was muttering softly to himself. "Hurry, hurry, hurry."

"I am, Jimmy," she murmured, even though she knew he wasn't talking to her.

When she returned to the tunnel a third time, she found

Helen Lawlor and two others already standing there. Patrick had discovered that he could herd them by using the torch. They instinctively shied away from the flames.

Pushing past the three girls, Claire joined Patrick in the central chamber.

"Start counting them," Patrick called. "We don't want to leave anyone behind."

"I've taken two out." She waved her torch at Christy Gunn, backing him towards the tunnel. "There's three in the tunnel – four," she added as the boy joined the others. "That's five in total."

"I'll try to get them into the tunnel, and you keep them there," Patrick shouted. He jabbed the flaming torch at Susan Beatty and Martin Simms, driving them both back. The boy stumbled and the flames licked the edge of his arm. He didn't even look at the burn.

"Seven," Claire called. "Hurry, Patrick, hurry." She waved the torch across the entrance to the tunnel as the students began pressing back in. The flickering flame crisped curls and singed hair, but they moved back.

"Nine," she called when they manoeuvred Fergus Conroy and Brenda Boyne into the tunnel. Now only two remained: Miss Lee and Tommy Butler. They were both burrowing at the ground, ignoring the flames which came dangerously close to them.

"Patrick – your torch!" Claire called.

Patrick suddenly realised that his torch had burned down to little more than a stub. Tendrils of petrol had trickled on to his hand, but he had been so intent on getting his friends out that he hadn't even felt it. Catching Tommy by the arm, he hauled him to his feet and shoved him violently towards the entrance. The boy took two steps and turned back.

Patrick looked into his friend's eyes, and saw that they were empty, that there was nothing there – no recognition, no emotion. Only the boy's lips moved, mimicking the whispering that hissed around the walls. "*Hurry*." Dragging him by the arm, Patrick pulled him into the tunnel with the others. Away from the centre of the chamber, he looked just slightly more alert, and was aware enough to move away from the torch.

Patrick returned for Miss Lee. Terrified, he saw that she had dug quite deep into the earth, clawing up handfuls of gritty soil. Catching her arm he pulled her to her feet and dragged her towards the tunnel. "Get them all out of here," he shouted to Claire.

"What are you going to do?" Claire demanded, realising that he wasn't coming with her.

"I'm going to fill in this hole."

Chapter Thirty-one

"Where's Patrick?" Nathan called, when Claire finally emerged from the tunnel behind the crowd of confused and sluggish students and teacher.

"He stayed behind to fill in the hole."

"Get him out. Get him out," Nathan Keeper was almost frantic. "The god is close to the surface. So close I can feel him. You have to get Patrick out, or the god will feed off him."

"You'll need this to control them," Claire lifted the sputtering remnants of her torch.

"You'll need it to find your way inside. I'll hold them back," the old man said. "Now go. Go!"

Claire ducked back into the tunnel, leaving Nathan Keeper with the milling blank-eyed students. Without the flame to control them, they all instinctively turned and headed back towards the tunnel. The old man positioned himself in their way, spreading his arms to block the entrance. They crowded around him, not striking him, simply pushing, pushing, pushing. Nathan caught the nearest boy and shoved him away, but the boy simply got to his feet and advanced on the old man again. Gripping the edge of the stone, Nathan attempted to halt their advance, but slowly, slowly, he was pushed into the opening, his fingernails leaving long scratch marks on the stone. He turned his head, hoping to see the approaching light as Patrick and Claire returned, but the tunnel remained in darkness. The mass of bodies pressed him deeper into the mound.

Patrick was dumping stones into the centre of the hole when Claire burst into the chamber. The whispering had died away to a dull incomprehensible muttering, angry and sullen. "We've got to get out of here."

"I must fill this in," Patrick said grimly.

"It's too late, Patrick. Too late." There were tears streaming down her face. "We've failed."

Patrick shook his head defiantly. "No, we haven't." He staggered beneath the weight of a heavy boulder, lugging it to the edge of the hole. Dropping it on the ground, he shoved it with his foot, and it rolled down into the centre. It shifted, settled, shifted again.

"Patrick, come on! Please. Nathan says the god is close to the surface."

Patrick dropped another rock into the hole.

The whispering stopped and the stench of putrefaction suddenly filled the chamber, driving Patrick and Claire back, coughing and gagging.

And an immense hand broke through the centre of the floor.

Gnarled and twisted, with flesh the colour of a bruise, the

fingers clawed the air, black nails scraping the ceiling. A second hand appeared, punching up from beneath the ground. The whole chamber trembled, stones grating, rocks falling, and then the floor split, torn apart as a dome of purple flesh appeared.

The head was hairless and almost completely round. There were no ears, two tiny indentations for nostrils, and the mouth was a ragged teeth-filled maw. A forked tongue flickered, tasting the air. And its eyes, when it opened them, were blood-red and slit-pupilled. They swivelled and fixed on the teenagers. The beast filled the chamber, more and more of it appearing from the ground, long purple serpent-like coils of flesh that shimmered with an oily irridescence.

"I am Crom Cruach. God of Gods.
Lord of this world."

The voice was a rumbling, hissing thunder that pounded in their heads.

"And you have sided with the priest,
which makes you fools."

The huge taloned claw rose suddenly, reaching for Patrick.

Claire jabbed at it with the torch, the flames licking at the creature's oily flesh, burning with a blue flickering flame. Crom Cruach hissed appallingly. It slashed at them, its nails carving a groove in the wall, slashed at them again, as Patrick struck it with the final remnants of his torch.

"Back, Claire," he said desperately, "go back." Holding his torch before him, he started to inch his way back down the tunnel. The god wouldn't be able to reach him here.

Like a huge slug, Crom Cruach dragged himself forward

on his claw-like hands ... and then his tongue flickered out, wrapping around Patrick's leg, catching him off balance, dropping him heavily to the ground, driving the breath from his body. His torch fell from his hands, and died in the dirt.

Patrick scrabbled frantically for a hand-hold as he was slowly dragged down the tunnel. He hadn't got the breath to cry out. He beat at the creature's tongue wrapped around his leg. It felt like rubber, and coated his hands in thick slime. His questing fingers caught on a rock. Holding on desperately, he felt the muscles in his leg and thigh stretch, the bones in his ankle creak under the pressure. Opening his mouth, he managed to scream, "Claire!" before the rock gave way and he was wrenched into the chamber with the god.

Crom Cruach towered over him, mouth gaping, claws slowly opening and closing.

"First I will take your soul ... then I will feast off your flesh!"

And then suddenly Claire was in the chamber, waving the torch to a sparking blaze. She jabbed it into the creature's flesh, oily blue flames dancing on his skin, jabbed it again and again, dozens of small fires burning on the god's flesh, while it roared and howled and rippled in agony. Patrick climbed shakily to his feet, pulled off the remains of his jacket and stuck a sleeve in the flame of Claire's torch and then, when the coat was burning fiercely, he threw it on to the god. The leather jacket wrapped itself around the creature's arm, sticking to him, the purple skin bubbling, burning with a dreadful smell.

Patrick shouted in triumph, until the god's flickering

tongue struck him across the head, knocking him to the ground.

And then the god caught Claire across the side, sending her crashing into the wall. The torch fell from her hand ... and the god's claw crushed it to splinters, plunging the chamber into darkness.

> *"Enough of these games. It is over for you now. But for me this is just the beginning ..."*

Patrick crawled over to Claire. His fingers touched hers and their hands locked together. They couldn't see, but they could feel Crom Cruach, huge above them, jaws gaping, claws ready to slash and rend.

"Patrick," Claire whispered, "I'm sorry ..." she began.

"So am I ..." he began, then stopped and stared. He could actually see the pale outline of her face. She was looking over his shoulder at Crom Cruach. "Claire?" he said. "Claire! I can see you ..." he said in wonder.

"Sunrise," she breathed.

The god's head descended.

And sunlight lanced through the light-box.

The cold pure light played across the god's purple-black skin. The flesh dried, seared and blackened, breaking away in huge sooty flakes. The enormous red eyes paled and hardened, then the liquid steamed away, the flickering tongue withering to a blackened stump. When the head hit the ground at the teenagers' feet, it shattered into dust.

Chapter Thirty-two

They found Nathan Keeper in the tunnel. He lay buried beneath the bodies of their unconscious friends. Patrick and Claire dragged the students off, pulling them out into the fresh air, and eased the old man into a sitting position. In the wan light of the morning sunshine, they could see that he was ageing before their eyes.

"I held them back," he whispered.

"The god is dead," Claire said simply. "The sun destroyed it."

"All those years in the ground had weakened it," Patrick said gently, "all those years you renewed the spell sapped its power. That, along with this last effort was too much."

The skin was tightening on the old man's face, turning it skull-like. "Your courage destroyed the Great Evil this time. Your courage – and your love." His voice was like a whisper. "But you must remember, that which does not live, cannot die. The god will re-appear some time, some place. And you must be ready. Now you are the Keepers."

"Keepers of what?" Patrick asked.

"Keepers of the human race."

Later, much later, as they watched the police cars and ambulances appear, sirens wailing down the narrow country roads, Patrick turned to Claire. "How are we going to explain all this?" he asked.

OTHER WORLD SERIES

OCTOBER MOON
Michael Scott

Rachel Stone and her family are scared by weird happenings at their stables in Kildare. But is it the locals trying to get rid of them or something more sinister? £3.99 pb

GEMINI GAME
Michael Scott

BJ and Liz O'Connor are gamemakers, but when their virtual reality computer game *Night's Castle* develops a bug, they risk their lives to try to solve the problem. An exciting futuristic novel. £3.99 pb

MOONLIGHT
Michael Carroll

Moonlight is not just an ordinary horse. His owner dreams he will be the fastest racehorse ever. But Cathy intervenes, and the result is a tense, nail-biting chase for survival. £3.99 pb

OTHER BOOKS FROM THE O'BRIEN PRESS

THE HUNTER'S MOON
Orla Melling

Adventure, mystery, and the sorcery and magic of the Other World combine when Findabhair disappears and her cousin Gwen sets out to find her. £3.99 pb

THE DRUID'S TUNE
Orla Melling

Caught up in the enchantments of a modern-day druid, Rosemary and Jimmy are hurled into the ancient past. They have the adventure of their lives in the unusual company of Cuchulainn and Queen Maeve. £4.50 pb

CELTIC MAGIC TALES
Liam Mac Uistin

Four magical legends from Ireland's Celtic past: the Tuatha de Danann and their king's love-quest; a fantastic and humorous tale of Cuchulainn; the story of Deirdre and the Sons of Usnach; the heroic tale of the Sons of Tuireann. £3.99 pb

AMELIA
Siobhán Parkinson

The year is 1914 and there are rumours of war in the air. But all that matters to Amelia is what she will wear to her thirteenth birthday party. But when disaster strikes her family, Amelia's life changes. £3.99 pb

STAR DANCER
Morgan Llywelyn

When Ger breaks into the RDS horse show, he sees a new world, and he desperately wants to be part of it. Suzanne, riding her horse Star Dancer, has a target too: she wants to train for the Olympics. Their dreams overlap, with interesting results. £3.99 pb

STRONGBOW
Morgan Llywelyn

The dramatic story of the arrival in Ireland of the Normans, and of Strongbow's life with his new wife, the young Irish princess Aoife. Vivid and exciting history with a strong story. £3.99 pb

BRIAN BORU
Morgan Llywelyn

The most famous of Ireland's heroes – this is his life story from childhood to the Battle of Clontarf. £3.95pb

UNDER THE HAWTHORN TREE
Marita Conlon-McKenna

The heartfelt, dramatic account of the children of the Great Irish Famine – Eily, Michael and Peggy – who make a long journey on their own to find the great-aunts they have heard about in their mother's stories. £3.95 pb

WILDFLOWER GIRL
Marita Conlon-McKenna

Peggy, now thirteen, sets out for America to find a new life. She goes into service in a large Boston house, and must find her own feet in the difficult world of the emigrant. £4.50 pb

THE BLUE HORSE
Marita Conlon-McKenna

When Katie's family's home burns down they are left destitute. Now she must find a way to hold the family together and must try to fit into a completely new life. But will she be accepted? £3.99 pb

HORSE THIEF
Hugh Galt

Rory's old horse is stolen, and to prevent it happening again he runs away with her in the night. But they soon come across another horse hidden in the depths of the country. Then begins the wildest chase, in an attempt to save both horses. £3.99 pb

THE LOST ISLAND
Eilís Dillon

Is the lost island real or fantasy? And who is brave enough to try to find it and gain the treasure? Michael and Joe set off on their boat to reveal the secret of the island. £3.95 pb

THE CRUISE OF THE SANTA MARIA
Eilís Dillon

John sets sail in a splendid Galway hooker, ending up on a deserted island, empty except for one unusual inhabitant. Here begins a strange adventure, full of excting, tense moments. £4.50 pb

........................Cut here..

ORDER FORM

Please send me the books as marked

I enclose cheque / postal order for £.........(+ 50p P&P per title) **OR**

please charge my credit card ☐ Access / Mastercard ☐ Visa

Card number ☐☐☐☐ ☐☐☐☐ ☐☐☐☐ ☐☐☐☐

expiry date ☐ ☐ ☐ ☐

Name _____ Tel: _____

Address _____

_____

Please send orders to : The O'Brien Press, 20 Victoria Rd, Dublin
Tel: (01) 923333 Fax: (01) 922777